INDIAN MUTINY

Hanuman Singh,
India, 1857-1858

by Pratima Mitchell

◼SCHOLASTIC

This book is for my dearest mother, Shakuntala Bhatia

While the events described and some of the characters in this book may be based
on actual historical events and real people, Hanuman Singh is a fictional character,
created by the author, and his story is a work of fiction.

Scholastic Children's Books
Commonwealth House, 1–19 New Oxford Street,
London, WC1A 1NU, UK
A division of Scholastic Ltd
London ~ New York ~ Toronto ~ Sydney ~ Auckland
Mexico City ~ New Delhi ~ Hong Kong

Published in the UK by Scholastic Ltd, 2002

ISBN 0 439 98108 5

Printed and bound in Great Britain by Mackays of Chatham Limited, Chatham, Kent
Cover image: With thanks to Hemlata Jain.
Cover background image: Hulton Getty.

2 4 6 8 10 9 7 5 3 1

The right of Pratima Mitchell to be identified as the author of this work has been
asserted by her in accordance with the Copyright, Designs and Patents Act, 1988.

1859

It seems very far away and long ago when I dreamed of joining the Bengal Army as a sowar – a cavalry soldier – to work with the British, the conquerors of my country. It used to be a great thing to be part of the Bengal Army, but all that changed after the uprisings. I, too, have changed and don't hanker after soldiering any more. What used to be my ambition died more than twelve months ago. No, I don't wish to join any army. I will be very content to follow in the footsteps of my father, and be a Thakur – a landowning yeoman farmer – here in Digna, in the province of Bundelkhand, when I am older.

It was two years ago, in the month of May, when I left my family and my village, and went away to Jhansi town. For years, I'd been dreaming of excitement, of new places and new sights; but what I saw and experienced made me old before my time. Listen – stories of war and blood only sound exciting when you hear them in ballads. The reality is closer to hell.

In those days, I had a friend in Jhansi with a gift for

making up songs about what was happening around us. He sang these songs when we shared an evening meal in the palace stables. His ballads were about people and battles and the winds of change. The words throb in my ears like muffled drumbeats when I think of him. Sometimes, I sing his songs to our villagers, as they are part of me now, buried for ever in my heart and mind.

Here then, is my story, set in the years of the Indian Mutiny. I tell it as I witnessed it in one small part of our vast country...

My story begins during the terrible drought and famine of 1833, many years before my birth. My father, Thakur Channa Singh, the Headman of our village, told me about many of our neighbours and their cattle, and how they had wasted away like blighted thorn trees. My family survived that famine. We were among the few, the lucky ones, who didn't owe money to the moneylender – the *mahajan*. We had managed to keep a goodly portion of our land to grow *bajra*, millet and vegetables. We had acres in plenty and, being of a proud Rajput caste, we didn't have to follow everything the English Collector sahib ordered us to do. My father told me that he was a big, red-faced man, always sweating. When he hauled himself up on his horse, he made a noise like the horse – *hrrmph*.

The sahib, Mr Morland, showed my father a map of the district and the amount of tax each farmer would have to pay the English government. "They must plant cotton," he said. "It's an order. That is what the English mills need and this is how much the return will be." But then, Father told me, the price of cotton slumped in the world market. The rains failed for the second year running, and no one could eat cotton. As I said, Father is clever; he had managed to keep some of our land for food, and so we had enough to feed us in the difficult years. We had our own wells, cows, buffaloes, fields. My sisters and cousins and female relatives were strong, healthy women, and the menfolk had been soldiers in the Company Bahadur in the Bengal Army for generations. We were dependent on no one.

Saleem's family was not so fortunate. Saleem was my friend from the cradle; we used to chase monkeys away from the new corn with our slingshots (I'm named after the monkey god, Hanuman, so I never hurt the creatures). But, in 1849, Saleem's parents had to sell their land because they had run up huge debts to pay for seed; they owed Mr Morland tax and the moneylender interest.

Once you tumble down to the bottom of the ladder, it's very hard to climb up again. Soon, it became a question of starvation for them all. Saleem's parents were faced with a terrible choice, and in the end they took Saleem and his older sister to the missionary station in Dattia. That was in 1852, when Saleem was ten. I was two years younger. I remember Saleem's mother, Aminabai, crying after she had come back from leaving her children with the missionaries – tears poured down her cheeks like the waters of the River Betwa.

"Oh, *behan*, oh, sister," she sobbed to my mother, and my mother began to cry as well. "We begged the white padre – take our son and daughter. You can convert them into Christians if you will have mercy and save their lives. It's better they become *kaffirs* than die like dogs in the dirt. May Allah forgive me! My heart is broken, broken into pieces."

Saleem's name changed to Christopher Masih. He was clever and quickly learned to read and write English, after which he trained to be a drummer boy in the Bengal Army. He saw battles and many exciting campaigns. He beat his drum to keep time for foot soldiers. I know because my older brother, Sewak Singh, who was a sepoy, a foot soldier, had marched behind the military band many times and spotted Saleem among the other musicians.

Oh, my brother, my brother, so tall and strong and handsome. There was no one like him in the entire district – in the entire world, I think. Sewak Singh, Sepoy in *Hotey ka Paltan*, 12th Bengal Native Infantry Regiment stationed in Nowgaon, district Hamirpur,

Bundelkhand, Central India, the World, the Universe. A red coat, he wore, with gold buttons, and a tall hat with pompoms, on his head. On his right shoulder, he rested a musket, called a Brown Bess. Always, he had a collection of new stories about his life in the barracks: his companions, the English officers and soldiers, their Commanding Officer, Colonel Ridley, whom the whole company worshipped because he was brave and fair to all the men.

My brother's regiment had fought in many wars – the Afghan Wars in Afghanistan and the two Sikh Wars in Panjab. In Panjab, the Sikh Maharajah and his soldiers all had Singh as their second name. It means "lion", and my brother said that they were the best fighting soldiers he had seen. (Even though our name is also Singh, we are Hindu Rajputs.)

My brother fought in the Battle of Gujarat in 1849, when the Sikhs were defeated by the British and Panjab was added to the map of British India. He once told me that, during a lull in the fighting, he was trying to snatch an hour or two of sleep, when suddenly his company was overwhelmed by a group of Sikh soldiers. Sewak Singh managed to snatch up his sword, but to his utter amazement, his Sikh opponent grabbed the razor-sharp blade with his bare hand and tore it away from my brother. Then the two fought a hand-to-hand combat, although the Sikh's hands were a mass of blood. Sewak Singh said that he had never been so frightened by a man's strength before. If one of his British officers hadn't come up from behind and bayoneted the Sikh soldier, my brother wouldn't have lived to tell the tale.

It was a long and fierce battle. When it was all over, the Sikhs put down their arms and handed over their kingdom to the British. Sewak Singh was there when the young prince, Dalip Singh, stepped down from his throne and gave a golden casket to the Governor General. In the casket was the fabulous Koh-in-Noor diamond. "Spoils of war," Sewak Singh told me, "but they should have left the diamond in India." Instead, it was carried to the Maharani Victoria across the *Kala Pani* – the Black Water.

Many of my brother's friends in the regiment were extremely particular about their caste, what they ate and drank, and whom they ate and drank with. Most people I know are the same because they are very strict about their religion. But my father believes that God does not worry about ritual and ceremony – He looks at what is inside a person. If our family wasn't so relaxed about such things, I wouldn't have been allowed to play with Saleem, a Muslim. Nor would Aminabai have been allowed within yards of my mother's kitchen.

Sewak Singh had another story that told of a badly wounded foot soldier, left for dead after a campaign. The man crawled inside a Muslim saint's tomb in the countryside to hide, until a passing Gujjar shepherd heard him moaning in agony. The shepherd brought him water and the soldier survived, but had to leave the Army because he was so disabled. On returning home, he was first greeted as a hero; but then his village priest heard that he owed his life to a low-caste shepherd boy. A most terrible *hullah* there was – as a high-caste Hindu, he'd taken water from a low-caste shepherd! Only after many ritual cleansing rites was the soldier allowed to take a normal part in village life again.

But sometimes soldiers were forced through circumstance to do things that were polluting to their persons. For instance, something truly disgusting had happened in Behrampur in the spring of the year the Mutiny began: a new rifle was imported from England, called the Enfield rifle. The cartridges were wrapped in paper, which had to be torn off by the teeth before they could be inserted in the gun. But – and my brother made me swear an oath that I wouldn't breathe a word to anyone in our family – the paper had been greased with lard and pig's fat. Even in our easy-going household that wouldn't be tolerated! Pork is strictly forbidden to Muslims and beef to Hindus! Some soldiers were very angry that the English sahibs did not care about their feelings on such a matter, so they refused to use the bullets. Even though the cartridge papers were changed, most soldiers wouldn't believe their officers and they still rejected the bullets. They were punished for their disobedience, and were even court-martialled and dismissed in disgrace. My brother said that there had been a rumour that it was a plot to convert all soldiers to Christianity, by first making them lose caste. What an impossible situation that would have been, to be a stranger and outcaste in your own family and village…

I played in the fields, took the cows to graze and swam in the village pond, just like all the other small boys. We went to our little school, where we were beaten for not learning our lessons, but we quickly forgot our punishments because there was always a game of *gulli-danda* going in the lanes and catapults to fire at pigeons and parrots.

Besides the very humdrum life of an ordinary boy, I had a window into the world beyond our village, through listening to my brother's stories. The Army was his life because he loved travel and adventure and excitement – he couldn't bear village life because it was so predictable and dull. The more I heard about his life outside our village world, the more I resolved to join up as soon as I reached the age of sixteen. Saleem's fate had decreed that he would be part of the wider world and I wanted to make sure that I wasn't left outside it!

March – June 1857

Then, out of the blue, a cousin who worked in the Palace of Jhansi – about 20 miles west of our village – sent a message to my father. His employer, the Rani of Jhansi, had asked him to find a *khidmutgar*, or guardian, to take care of her eight-year-old adopted son, Damodar Rao. The child was lonely and in the company of women all day – his father had been dead for four years. He needed the companionship of an older, responsible boy to do things with – to go riding, to practise fencing and games.

So suddenly, the wider world seemed to be beckoning me! The possibility that I might leave Digna and the life I had known was a reality. Me, live in the royal palace in Jhansi? It was like a fairytale. A few weeks later, another message arrived, telling me to present myself at court for an interview. Rani Lakshmibai and her father, Moro Pant, wanted to size me up. The Rani saw me face-to-face, since I was too young for her to worry about a veil, which all high-born married ladies wear.

"Look at his eyes," she remarked to her father. "They look kind. How many children are you in the family, Hanuman Singh?"

"Four, Your Highness."

She looked approving.

Her father said, "I am more interested in his muscles." He squeezed my right arm like he was feeling a mango for ripeness. "You have to be strong enough to protect my grandson."

For most of the interview, I kept my eyes on the ground, but I could not help noticing the lady's face: round, quite dark-skinned, with large, sparkling eyes outlined with kohl, and a necklace of pearls round her neck. She was about 30 years old and her head was covered with a muslin *dupatta* embroidered with silver thread.

Then she said, "You may go now. We will send for you when the time is right. Here, take this present for your mother." She gave me a silk purse. There was something hard inside. Afterwards, when I looked, I found that it carried three gold *mohurs*. My head was spinning with excitement. There were still two years to go before I could join the Army, but now, unexpectedly, my chance to leave our dusty village had arrived. I thought: I will work for the Rani until I am sixteen, and then I will enlist in the Bengal Army like my brother.

The palace was a wonderful, tall building with miles and miles of passages full of servants who hurried by soundlessly. Outside the palace gate, I looked back at the shuttered windows and the series of niches in the outer wall. Almost all were occupied by guards, or people who had travelled distances to ask the Rani for favours. One of these days, I thought, I will be a privileged courtier, part of the royal household. I felt very superior.

In May, the hot weather was upon us and a spiteful wind was spitting fire from the desert. We were expecting Sewak Singh to come home on leave to see his baby son, my nephew, for the first time. I was bursting like an overstuffed sack of wheat with all the questions I was going to ask him. I could picture his arrival, and I knew where I'd be – up the tamarind tree that grew beyond the mud walls of our village. It was a great lookout for me and my friends. Lessons with the village priest could wait. I imagined how I would scan the horizon for the first tell-tale cloud of dust.

Sewak Singh usually travelled some of the way in an *ikka*, a high two-wheeled pony cart, and then walked cross-country to our village of Digna.

After folding up his red coat and putting away his boots, my brother would have a purifying bath and be blessed by the priest in the temple. Only then would he greet my mother, my father, his wife and their children. I couldn't wait to hear the latest news about the bullets and other matters from Sewak Singh.

My soldier brother was supposed to arrive on a Monday or Tuesday, though Tuesday was not a good day, being unlucky for travellers. Anything could happen – a snake could cross your path, a tiger could spring out of the jungle, a gang of thugs could ambush you, your shoes might fall apart, your head could be attacked by sunstroke… The list of possible disasters was endless.

On Monday morning, I started my lessons with the priest and the other boys under the *neem* tree near the temple. Our teacher set us verses to memorize from the *Ramayana*. When there was a pause during his droning, I spoke up.

"My head aches," I said, screwing up my eyes and holding my head dramatically. The priest regarded me shrewdly. "Your brother is expected today, isn't he?

16

Be off with you then, but come prepared with those verses tomorrow." I pretended to be offended and got up with exaggerated care and small groans, but as soon as I was out of sight I took to my heels and pelted down the lane to the village gate. I chucked my whitened slate and reed pen under a *datura* bush and ran the remaining mile to the tamarind tree, my lookout. In an instant, I was up in its branches, with a fine view over the countryside.

On my right, I saw a gleam of silver where the River Betwa ran in the direction of our neighbouring state, Orchha. Its shallows were teeming with *rohu* fish, which swam trustingly near us when we bathed. In front of me was mile after mile of scrubland, dotted with small clumps of thorn trees, poisonous *datura* and pampas grass. The landscape was a maze of deep ravines of ochre-yellow earth and outcrops of black rock, excellent hiding places for the thugs and robbers that roamed the countryside. The heat was making floating mirages of lakes and castles in the distance and soon my eyes started throbbing. Patiently, I watched for the cloud of dust that would proclaim my brother's arrival. The heat and the crickets had almost hypnotized me to sleep when I was jolted to my senses again – what was that flash to my left? I squinted through the leaves and saw a column of men, half a mile away, raising puffs of dust, and moving in the direction of where I sat. Their voices travelled on the lift of a breeze, which set the ripe tamarind fruit clattering lightly above me. I shrank back to be less visible and flattened myself against the branch. A little way from my perch was a well, overhung by a *kikar* tree. They seemed to be making for that. There were six of them, five of them youngish and one old man with a long beard. They were covered in white dust and looked exhausted. One of them had a Brown Bess rifle on his back. I could hear their conversation quite distinctly.

"We will reach my village by nightfall," said Greybeard, "and then we will be safe. My kinsfolk will hide us from the police and the English."

"What rubbish you talk, old man," said one of the younger ones. "Who should we hide from now? The *Angrez* are finished. Their rule has come to an end. Everyone knows that and there is nothing to worry about."

"If that's the case, then why are we sneaking about the countryside and looking for a safe place?"

Another man growled, "The *Angrez* are going back to their own country. That is what the prophecy says,

18

doesn't it? That the foreigner's rule would last a hundred years after the Battle of Plassey and end in June 1857."

A fourth man spoke with emphasis. "Every villager we have come across knows this is a true saying. Those *chapattis* that are being passed around the northern provinces – there is a reason for this. It means just what Chaubey just said – the fulfilment of the prophecy."

I clapped my hand to my mouth to stop myself joining in their talk. The *chapattis*! Some weeks earlier, the runner who had come from the town of Orchha had handed my father, the Headman of our village, two stale grubby pieces of flat bread.

"All I know is that I was supposed to give them to you," he had panted. "I know nothing more. You must send two more with a runner to the next district, or else you will be plagued with bad luck." My father threatened to beat the truth out of the runner, but he only said, "Save your beating for someone else. All I have heard is that something is going to happen to the *Angrez*." Now here were these strangers discussing that very topic!

Greybeard hauled up water from the well and drank thirstily. He wiped his mouth. "Come on lads, let's hurry on. I haven't seen my family for three years, not

since the English pigs jailed me for deserting the Army."
He re-wound his dirty turban and picked up his pack.

I suddenly felt a sneeze coming on and, before I
could stop it, "Atishoo!" There was nothing for it now
but to declare myself, so I shinned down the tree and
found myself facing the menacing barrel of a musket.

"Leave him alone," Greybeard said. "He's only a
village boy."

The armed man snapped, "To whom will you
betray our whereabouts? Are you a serf of the Rani of
Orchha? She is a bitch of the English and Orchha state
is their lapdog."

Larai Rani of Orchha was no friend to my future
employer, the Rani of Jhansi. Orchha and Jhansi had
been on snarling terms with one another for generations.

"Oh, no, Your Grace." I folded my hands. Best keep
quiet about Sewak Singh, I thought. I prayed fervently
that he wasn't about to appear on the horizon, because
as a loyal soldier of the Bengal Army he would have to
arrest these men. If he arrived dressed in his red coat,
they might fire the musket at him. Then again if,
happily, their paths didn't cross, he would want to
know about them. I decided to find out more.

"I am the younger son of Thakur Channa Singh of
Digna." I spoke like a village innocent. "I just

happened to overhear you." I thought it best to disarm them by admitting that I had heard their talk. "I am curious to know what brings you here."

"What were you doing up the tree?"

"Scanning the horizon for a herd of straying goats, Your Honour," I lied.

Greybeard wasn't suspicious. He took the trouble to give me an explanation.

"A veritable fire has erupted in the Army in Meerut town. It spread to Lucknow last month. Hindu and Muslim soldiers have risen up against the British and marched to Delhi. We last heard that Delhi was under siege and that Bahadur Shah Zafar, the old Mughal Emperor who was put out to grass by the foreigner, has been declared Padshah – the Emperor of India – again. We were freed by our fellow soldiers from jail in Lucknow and now we are going somewhere safe. Soon, the English will be driven into the Bay of Bengal to drown and, praise God, we will be rid of them for ever! So farewell, young lad, and keep your mouth shut about where we are heading…"

His companions whooped like maniacs, laughing loudly. Then they picked up their bundles and moved on, soon disappearing in to the maze of ravines, heading in the direction of Lalitpur.

Forgetting all about watching out for Sewak Singh, I ran as fast as I could back to our village and burst in to my father's room, where he was doing his accounts with his *munshi*.

It was so reassuring to see him and hear the familiar, high-pitched voice of the bald clerk after my strange encounter with the jailbirds. "The *Angrez* are finished! They have left our country!" I gasped, before launching into an account of what I had seen and heard.

Father looked grave. "Maybe those *chapattis* did mean something."

Munshiji piped up in his reedy voice, "The priest had a dream last night of rivers of blood and Jhansi in flames. He told me that the stars show a terrible period of death and destruction. The planet Rahu always brings carnage and violence in its wake."

"Let us reserve judgement until your brother comes from Jhansi," said Father. "He will surely bring the true state of affairs." He waved his hand in dismissal. "Go, go and climb your tree and see if Sewak Singh is on his way."

It was cow-dust time when he eventually arrived – the time of evening when the cattle kick up dust as they are driven home from pasture. I proudly relieved Sewak Singh of his gun and said a hasty, "Ram Ram" to the coolie who was carrying the rest of his luggage. My brother's packhorse didn't bother returning my good wishes. His eyes stayed fixed on the ground and no word emerged from his mouth. The lower part of his face was swathed in a greyish cloth and on his head was a country turban. Even though the May heat must have been bubbling like the devil's cauldron inside his grubby garments, he did not seem to trust an inch of his limbs to exposure. Even his feet were covered, way above his ankles. To my surprise they were wrapped in big *tendu* leaves. Only beggars who have walked a very long way do that to their feet.

My brother ignored the coolie's bad manners and placed his arm around my shoulders as we stepped in rhythm along the homeward path. The light was fading by the second, but when I glanced up at Sewak Singh's face it was a shock to see new worry lines on his forehead. Just before we entered the village through the heavy, studded gates, he stopped and turned me around to look into his sombre eyes.

"Tomorrow morning at the crack of dawn, you will leave for Jhansi. The Rani has sent for you and you must go immediately. I will follow in a week or so, after seeing the baby and doing some business with Father. I have another task for you – a very important one. You must take my friend here," he indicated the coolie who was squatting on his haunches, "safely to Orchha." The coolie raised his head for the first time to look directly at me. To my utter astonishment, when I met his eyes they were blue like the sky!

My brother then told me things that, even in that furnace-like heat, turned my blood to ice. I had already heard some of these stories, but they hadn't seemed real until I heard them from my own brother. He spoke very quickly in a low, urgent voice. He said that a terrible wave of violence and rebellion had broken out in the Army. From a small mutiny in Meerut – just three regiments – his fellow sepoys had gone on a rampage of destruction; they and many outside the Army had killed English officers and civilians – men, women and children. The Meerut soldiers were now in Delhi and had proclaimed the old Mughal Emperor to be Padshah of India again.

Sewak Singh jerked his head at the coolie. "He is an *Angrez* sahib. He managed to escape from Delhi and he's been in hiding. He has been travelling across the country to find a safe haven since his fellow officers were killed in the Delhi siege. There were very few English to fend off the attack from the sepoys, and the telegraph was cut off. Not all of us Indian soldiers are for killing the British; certainly I am not, so I feel, as he is my guest, I must protect him."

I related what the jailbirds had spoken about earlier that day.

"They don't know the half of it... Which way did they go?"

"South, in the direction of Lalitpur."

"Good. We don't want this poor man blasted by a shotgun. Make sure you take him all the way to the English Collector in the District Court. I think his name is Brown. Larai Rani of Orchha is also a friend of the English and she will protect him. Otherwise, I fear he might be murdered by thugs or some bloodthirsty soldiers."

"I'm confused, Bhaiya. Are you on the side of the soldiers or the English?"

My brother wiped his troubled brow with the back of his hand and, glancing briefly at the Englishman said, "I don't know, little brother. There's a part of me that wants to show the English whom our land belongs to, and another part of me that wants to serve in the company and regiment that I love. Sometimes, loyalty is a very difficult thing to pinpoint. Come, let's go into the house now, or people will start to wonder. After everyone is in bed, we'll talk again. Poole Sahib can sleep in the cowshed and you can take him food and water – he hasn't eaten much apart from forest berries and wild spinach."

Later that night, when the last *diya* flame had been pinched dead and the baby settled, my brother indicated that I should follow him. We sat by the door of the cowshed, away from the family, who were sleeping in the open air, shrouded against the night dew, under the stars. Poole Sahib was stretched out on clean straw inside the cowshed.

"No one must guess that Poole Sahib has been here or we'll be branded as traitors to the cause."

"And you, Bhaiya? Will you join the others? I don't understand why this is happening…" I said.

My brother whispered, "The Army is my life. I love my regiment and even my officers, who treat us like their children. But our pay is low – only seven rupees a month, and even the *batta* that we are paid for campaigns outside India may be stopped. There are good reasons for the sepoys' discontent. In fact, there is a lot of hatred for the *Angrez*. Then there is the feeling that our own kings and queens have been unfairly treated – humiliated and dispossessed. For instance, Rani Lakshmibai of Jhansi is not sovereign over her own lands – the British are. Lord Sahib

Dalhousie took away her rights because he didn't recognize her adopted son as heir. In Oudh, the British said that the Nawab wasn't fit to rule his kingdom. See here," he held up his right hand, "pretend this is our country – it's the shape of a palm. And all *this* territory is ruled by the British." He indicated a large part of his hand with his other forefinger. "Whose country is it now? Ours or theirs?"

Someone, I think it was my father, coughed and stirred on his string bed, a few yards away in the courtyard. My brother waited a while before continuing. "Then there's the matter of the land tax. It's so rough and ready – you know how many people it has crippled."

"Like Saleem's parents," I said.

"That's right. Oh, I nearly forgot to tell you … I saw him when I came through Jhansi. If the Jhansi troops revolt, then Saleem and other Christians will be in trouble. His sister, who was given to the missionaries, is working as an *ayah* for the District Commissioner's children. The rebel sepoys are intent on killing all Christian converts. There is a rumour that the British want to force us all to change our religion, which is why they greased the bullets with animal fat."

"Bhaiya, what are you going to do?"

"I haven't quite decided yet. I sympathize with my brother soldiers, but I don't want to kill anyone in cold blood. Also, I don't think it's wise to rebel against such a powerful master – this revolt will be put down in no time – the *Angrez* are very clever and very strong. They will spare no one who rises against them. But there is something else – Rani Lakshmibai of Jhansi has asked me to join her personal bodyguard, because she can't trust her troops. She needs to feel secure."

"Against the British? I thought she was on friendly terms with them."

"These days no one should count on friendship. She has always had good relations with them, but that doesn't mean she is loyal to the foreigner. The Rani will have to make a clear-cut political decision about which side she's on, sooner rather than later. Her soldiers won't leave her in peace otherwise."

"So she fears her soldiers?"

"Not only them; she has other enemies – the state of Orchha and other rivals who want their own man to replace Lakshmibai. Everyone knows that Larai Rani of Orchha has always said she'll take back Jhansi because it used to belong to her ancestors a long time ago. Now Orchha is firmly with the British because they want their backing." My brother yawned and rubbed his hand over his face. "But if I join Rani Lakshmibai, then I will effectively be deserting the Army – a very big step for me. But I feel sorry for her. She is a brave lady, which is why I agreed to let you serve her."

"I feel scared." I felt a shiver of apprehension. All of a sudden, the idea of leaving the safety of my home for an unknown and dangerous future was not attractive at all.

But my brother looked resolute. "I have given my word. I cannot let her down now. You have to learn to be a man. Her Highness lives in fear that her son may be poisoned or murdered by her enemies."

I nodded slowly, realizing for the first time the responsibility that had been laid on me. Instead of my former excitement at the thought of going away, a kind of heaviness weighed on my spirits.

My family was already resigned to my going, so my sudden departure the next morning wasn't a complete surprise. My two younger brothers came running in from the fields to see me off. They were round-eyed and unusually well-behaved, but the six-year-old made a face at me just as I set off. I made as if to hit him and he ran away giggling breathlessly. "Idiot!" I called after him.

My mother placed a little curd and a lump of brown sugar on my tongue to ward off evil and my little sister, who was eight, said solemnly, "Hanuman, Bhaiya, I want to know everything that happens. You won't forget anything, will you?" I held her by her arms and swung her up. "Ow, ow, you're hurting me!" she cried.

Sewak Singh and his wife embraced me and made their small boy wave goodbye. Sewak Singh suggested that I keep a note of what I saw and did, so the whole family would be able to share my exciting experiences. "You can put your learning to practical use," he said.

The coolie was waiting at the gateway to the village. He lifted my bundle on his head and, trotting a few paces behind me as coolies do, we set off on our journey. I glanced back for a last look at my family, then I turned my face towards my unknown fate and walked down the same path my brother had trodden only the evening before. I was very aware of the Sahib carrying my load. Once or twice, I nearly said something, but was too shy to address him; besides he didn't speak our language, did he, so what would I say? And what if the men from yesterday were hanging around somewhere? I knew they would have no mercy on Poole Sahib if they saw his blue eyes.

We walked for about two miles until we reached the main bullock track. This was used by us villagers to go to market and to the bigger places like Jhansi, and also by travelling salesmen, who came our way with trinkets, cloth and utensils. The track ran like a sandy tunnel between high embankments covered with pampas grass, twisting and turning in gullies all the way to Orchha. Around one such bend we saw a man appear, advancing at a steady pace. I gave Poole Sahib a warning look, but his eyes were fixed on the ground in front of his feet. I coughed loudly and spoke to the approaching stranger. "Ram Ram!"

I was relieved to see that he was only a faquir, a holy man, thin like the bamboo stave I was carrying. His eyes burned like hot coals and his body was smeared with white ash. He pointed his stick at me, shouting, "Turn back, turn back. Pestilence and war! The foreign devils are poisoning our food and water! Bones of cows and pigs are being mixed with flour. Did you ever dream of such a thing? No, never."

He shook the stick at the sky. "Brahma, Vishnu, Shivdev! Grant us strength to drive out the accursed English dogs!"

I bowed my head and made as though to touch his feet, then hurried on with Poole Sahib right behind me. I nearly jumped out of my skin when I suddenly heard his voice behind me. It was the first time I'd heard him speak.

31

"What madness has overtaken us all?" the English officer said in fluent Hindustani. He seemed glad to loosen his tongue. "Everyone I knew is dead. All my friends and fellow officers. Their wives and children, too. Lucky that I am single."

Now that the ice had been broken, my shyness somehow disappeared. Poole was another human being, a person who was feeling his way round a situation, just as I was. He continued speaking in a low tone, "I must telegraph the Governor in Bombay. You wouldn't know if the telegraph is functioning here, would you? No, of course not. The Collector will tell me. The Central Indian Field Force has to start out immediately from Bombay with thousands of troops. We British are defenceless in most of our cantonments, which is why things have got out of control. This mutiny won't be long in reaching us here and spreading all over India."

With a shock, I realized that these confidences were important information to the right persons. I felt uncomfortable. My only thoughts until now had been to please my brother by carrying out his orders and ensuring the Captain's safe passage. I was only conscious of my responsibility, and acutely aware that my soldier brother was in a muddle about which side he ought to support. Now it struck me – was this white sahib an enemy, or was he my brother's superior officer who had to be respected and obeyed?

At last, we reached the outskirts of Orchha town, a strange, spooky place full of the ghosts of the kings of Bundelkhand – with its ancient tombs and temples and memorials that loomed in the dusk like enormous sentries of the dead. Bats swooped down and around us, as we made our way to the Collector's bungalow. It was the first time I had seen an *Angrezi* house. It was a big, white, sprawling bungalow with a garden at the front and rear.

Poole Sahib pressed my hand. "Thank you," he said, and that was that. I saw him go up to the front door and heard him bellowing, "Brown! Brown! Open up, man! It's Captain Poole!" He disappeared inside, looking back at me just once to wave me on. I went round the back of the bungalow and the Collector's bearer signalled that I should come into his quarters. I spent the night on his floor and, having completed my job, next morning I hitched a ride on a bullock cart going to Jhansi and soon forgot about the sahib.

The carter woke me from my doze when we were on the outskirts of Jhansi. "Look, there is the military cantonment where the white sahibs live," he said, pointing with his whip. The settlement was too far away for me to see it properly, but a big fort in the cantonment was clearly visible. "That's the Star Fort," added the carter, "where the soldiers keep their arms and stores."

About quarter of an hour later and a mile further on, he dropped me and my bundle off at the bottom of a hill. Above us loomed the city wall that encircled Jhansi Fort, the old town and the Rani's palace. I climbed the rocky incline, heading towards the great blocks of reddish sandstone. Then, following the wall round, I found an open gate, higher and wider than an elephant. The guard wasn't visible and no one challenged me. Immediately inside the gate, I saw the open mouth of a massive, black, iron cannon. It would have wiped out Jhansi's enemies within minutes.

My next thought was that I must wash off the roadside dust and change into clean clothes before making my appearance at the palace. I saw to my right a narrow lane overhung with balconies, which disappeared into a maze of buildings. The lane wound its way through to the old part of the town, where I located the Ganesh temple. It had a well with a paved area next to it and I was soon sluicing water over myself. I cleaned my teeth with a *neem* stick, rubbed my hair dry and set off for the palace.

I retraced my steps back to where I had come in through the city gate and walked in the direction of the palace. It took a little while to convince the guard that I had been invited by the Rani herself. "Why don't you fetch my cousin? He'll vouch for me," I said in my humblest tone. After about an hour, my cousin arrived looking harassed and bustled me to my room, which was near the stables. It was nothing to write home about – just a room with a bed and two nails in the wall to hang my clothes on.

"Hurry, tidy up and present yourself to the Rani Sahiba," he fussed. I had never had warm feelings for my cousin, so I was quite pleased when he said that he was too busy to worry about me. There were hundreds of retainers and courtiers in the palace and, in fact, I rarely saw him after that first day.

I soon learned that the Rani wasn't one for small talk. After acknowledging my respectful greeting, she said, "I want my boy to be as tough as my Maratha ancestors. Train him to wrestle, like you do in the village, and to keep his saddle, and don't let him get fat and lazy and used to luxury." She had an abrupt, no-nonsense way of talking. At least I would know where I stood with her, I thought.

The little prince Damodar Rao's charms went only

as far as the dimple in his plump cheek. I had trouble getting him to listen to me. He was wilful and bad-tempered, because he was a spoiled child. If he didn't get his own way, he kicked and screamed until his eyeballs almost popped. The people in the palace told me that his mother had been very different at his age.

The Rani of Jhansi had been brought up almost like a boy in the household of the exiled Maratha ruler, the Peshwa Baji Rao II. Like the Sikhs, the Marathas were famed as soldiers; and like the Sikhs, the British had taken over their country and pensioned off their king, the Peshwa. If they didn't have sons to succeed them, Indian rulers would adopt boy children who would become their heirs. The Peshwa's adopted son was Nana Sahib.

Rani Lakshmibai's father, Moro Pant, was adviser to the Peshwa and the family lived in Gwalior until she was married off to a much older man, the Raja of Jhansi. As children, Lakshmibai, Nana Sahib and his friend, Tantia Topey, had been taught fencing, horse-riding and all kinds of sports. Their friendship was an old one.

Having given a little thought to the prince's welfare, I decided to improve his horsemanship by taking him riding every morning. It became our daily practice to set off, flanked by the Rani's famous women warriors from the battalion of female soldiers specially trained by her. Two female escorts rode a little behind us and, to tell the truth, I was more than a little frightened of them. Superb horsewomen, they had been trained never to smile. Straight-backed and stern, with lances erect, they rode astride, wearing Maratha-style saris tucked in between their legs just like pantaloons.

Shortly after my arrival at the palace – a week later to be exact – I was given a message from my brother saying that he would meet me early the next morning in the army cantonment, on his way back to his regiment, which was stationed in Nowgaon. Good, I thought. It wouldn't be difficult to arrange a meeting since I could combine this with our normal early-morning ride.

The next day, the young prince and I trotted sedately along the straight, tree-lined roads and I could just see over high hedges into the bungalow gardens – tidy and green with lawns, flowering jacaranda and *gul-mohur* trees. British officers lived in the army cantonment with their wives and families. It was a safe and orderly place, because they all knew and respected the Rani and thought of her as an ally. The soldiers' barracks were dotted around in the centre of the cantonment. Riding past one bungalow, I saw the door flung open and watched as pink-faced children chased a yellow puppy into the garden. I had only seen one other English person before – Captain Poole – and he was dark from his disguise. Liveried servants went in and out of the houses and a buggy with a Memsahib, wearing a strange-looking hat covered in flowers, passed us and turned into a gravelled drive. It was a peaceful place and no one gave us a second glance.

I thought that my brother was probably waiting near the parade ground, so I turned the prince's pony in that direction. A flag fluttered from a white pole on the vast *maidan* and a company of sepoys was marching smartly towards the Star Fort, which I knew housed the treasure and armoury. Four smart boys led the men, with a rat-tat-tat of drum and flourish of pipe music. I couldn't make out their faces from that far, but wondered if the drummer was my old friend Saleem, or Christopher.

We were some distance still when I halted our little procession to let the prince watch the soldiers. They marched in through the gates of the Star Fort, the sound of pipe and drum disappearing with them, and the gates closed.

"I'm hungry. I want to go home," whimpered the prince.

As I looked around wondering where my brother could be, a sharp and shocking volley of gunfire erupted from inside the Star Fort. The explosions continued, with little breaks in between. The noise was like the firecrackers we set off at the festival of *Dussehra*. The horses reared, rolling their eyes and whinnying, and our women escorts surrounded the prince. They shouted, "We must return immediately to the palace." But before we could turn the horses, a terrific hullabaloo broke out. Suddenly the peaceful cantonment was buzzing with activity like a live wasps' nest. The quiet tree-lined avenues were teeming with men. My heart started to thud and the prince began to wail, lifting his face to the sky in noisy hysterical sobs. "Shush, Your Highness, it's only a game," I scolded, not really believing my words. Soldiers were running here and there. Where, oh, where had my brother gone? In the confusion, I hardly noticed that his familiar figure was part of a group of red-jacketed soldiers who came running past us, streaming across the *maidan* towards the Star Fort. Then, to my great relief, I saw Sewak Singh separate from the other sepoys and make a dash for our little group.

"Quick!" he exclaimed. "Let's get out … there's trouble in the Star Fort."

The next thing I knew he had vaulted on to my horse's back behind me and was skilfully guiding the prince's horse and mine, cantering back the way we had come. The hooves thudded in time with my heart until we were safely up the hill that led to Jhansi Palace. I looked back quickly. One of the English bungalows was smoking. Could it be on fire? As soon as we were safely inside the gateway and clattering into the palace courtyard, Sewak Singh jumped off and ran indoors with a shout, "Take care of the prince. I must take vital news to the Rani!"

When the Rani finally sent for me, she had lifted her customary veil and was in deep consultation with my brother. Next to her stood her father, Moro Pant. The little prince hiccupped uncontrollably with fear. The Rani took his chin and looked steadily into his face. "We have just been told that the sepoys have taken over the Star Fort, which means they hold the guns, ammunition and treasure. There are hardly any *Angrez* in this area to prevent them. This is a state of emergency and we need to prepare ourselves. Queens and kings have to make difficult decisions and look after their kingdoms. You need to know these things if you are going to rule Jhansi one day."

The prince's eyes went as round as marbles and he started to suck his thumb. He was only a small boy. His eyes started to fill again, so I moved forward and held his hand.

My brother bowed. "Highness, the 12th Native Infantry seem to be modelling themselves on the soldiers in Meerut and Delhi. You must decide if you will side with them, or keep on the right side of the *Angrez*. I have to make the same decision, whether to throw in my lot with you, or head back to my unit in Nowgaon. If I go back, I may be forced to join the rebels, even if I don't care for their leader. Rissaldar Parvez Ahmed is no friend of mine."

The Rani's response was quick. "You are welcome to join me as a valued member of my personal bodyguard, although I will not ask you to do what is against your grain. But while you are still with us in the palace, I wish to be kept informed of *everything* that is happening within Jhansi town and in the cantonment and outlying areas…" She and my brother talked for some time about how he would organize a group of men to wander around picking up what news they could.

While they were discussing these matters, I heard a commotion in the passage outside – angry voices and sounds of scuffling. Alerted, the Rani held up her hand for silence among us. All of a sudden, soldiers wearing the red jackets of the Bengal Army trooped noisily into the *durbar* room, roughly pushing the Rani's ladies-in-waiting aside to get closer to the throne. One of them even had the nerve to grab the little prince by the shoulder. It all happened so quickly that we were powerless to stop them. They were heavily armed and there was nothing we could do except watch for their next move. Having jostled their way inside, they lined themselves up before the Rani.

"Rani Sahiba!" the leader barked rudely. "We need a decision from you. If you intend to help the English, we will accompany your old enemy the Larai Rani of Orchha to Jhansi and support her in taking over your kingdom. One thing we can promise – your son will be made a beggar and you will be put in prison. Don't force us to do that."

Moro Pant, my brother and the rest of the bodyguard exchanged outraged, helpless looks because they knew that the Rani's personal army was outnumbered by the rebel soldiers.

The Rani was furious. "Get out. Get out of my

palace! How dare you enter my dominion and threaten me in this vile way?" More noise and clanging of arms came from the corridor outside and a second group of soldiers entered, again roughly elbowing their way past the Rani's guards.

"The *Angrez* have all run inside Jhansi Fort, like mice being chased by a cat! Cowards they are, together with their servants and *syces*. Their supplies won't last long." The leader sneered. "This is the end for them. They have lynched our brothers in Delhi and Lucknow and fired them from cannons like human ammunition. We want revenge! We've destroyed their property in Jhansi! Their houses are burning merrily – death to the British!"

"Death to the British!" the others roared. The room had become very hot with all those extra bodies, and their voices broke like monsoon thunder.

Somehow, the Rani had managed to cool down a little. She was breathing quickly, but seemed more in control of herself. Her hands fluttered in gestures of pacification. "That is enough for now," she said. "You have made your point. Please leave and I will give you my decision in a day or two." As firmly as he dared, given the dangerous situation, my brother led the rebels to the door. The soldiers' leader turned to him and said mockingly, "So, you've deserted your regiment? At least you haven't run away and holed up with the English. Now use your influence over Rani Lakshmibai and make her see sense!"

Afterwards, the Rani, her father, ministers and my brother went into an inner room to weigh up the advantages and disadvantages of putting in their lot with the rebels. They sat up most of the night calculating what the cost might be.

I spent the night on a mat by Damodar Rao's bed, trying to get a little sleep. But it was impossible.

Two days later, early on the morning of 7 June, a body was discovered in the royal cowsheds. The man was dressed like a beggar and his face and hands were black with grime. In his cummerbund, they found a letter in English pleading with the Rani to send help to the English who were under siege in Jhansi Fort. It was the third day of the siege and no food was allowed from outside. When they undressed the beggar, they found he was an English officer, Captain Andrews. He had been murdered, either by the rebels or by someone in the palace who didn't want the letter to reach the Rani.

Later the same day, the rebel soldiers started firing guns at Jhansi Fort. The British retaliated from a raised terrace within. This went on for a couple of hours, then the guns went quiet and we heard no more. After that, there was an ominous silence the whole night long, apart from the hooting of owls, which always brings bad tidings.

Next day, 8 June, I went out into the courtyard of the palace. I was short on sleep and in a filthy mood. I muttered angrily to myself, which at least made me feel better. I fixed one end of a piece of rope to the nail in the wall and looked around for a post for the other end. I was arranging a high jump for the prince, as I had to think of ways to amuse him while we were cut off from the outside world. Since the trouble with the sepoys, the Rani had retreated with her court into the palace and secured the gates. Guards were posted and no one was allowed to come in without her direct permission. No more morning rides, no more walks into town to enjoy the hustle and bustle of the bazaar. We were stuck inside like prisoners. The palace didn't seem so beautiful and grand any more.

"I wish I'd never come. I wish I could run away home. I'm fed up with the stink of conspiracy and I can't stand the bad-tempered little brat," I grumbled under my breath. Then I remembered the British, who really were prisoners and whose lives were in danger. How much longer could they hold out against the sepoys? My thoughts flew to my old friend, Saleem. I wondered what he was doing. Had he managed to find his way back to the mission station, or to his parents in our village?

The day was hot, and bright like the brass pots that my mother scoured with ashes. The prince was taking his afternoon siesta. Soon, I would wake him up with a silver tumbler of cold *lassi*. It must have been two o'clock when I looked up at the sky (not something I do in the summer months) and I saw a most unusual sight for the month of June. Black clouds had gathered and a few minutes later they blotted out the sun. But my dark thoughts were broken by the sound of boots ringing out on the flagstones. I saw my brother striding out of the palace towards me, looking extremely agitated.

"Where have you been? I've been looking everywhere for you," he said crossly. "The British who were sheltering in Jhansi Fort have all been killed in Jhokun Bagh!" That was the garden just outside the fort. With a shudder, I remembered how ominously quiet it had become the night before. Sewak Singh went on, "I just heard that, this morning, a palace guard arrived at the fort with a message for the British Superintendant, Mr Skene. It said that Rani Lakshmibai had promised the British safe conduct back to their bungalows in the cantonment. They were all overjoyed, because their supplies had nearly run out." My brother looked down at the ground, very troubled. "But, Hanuman, I know for a fact that she gave no such promise. Out they came, ready to walk back to their homes and instead they were butchered." He frowned. "Captain Gordon, one of the senior officers, was shot dead – I knew him. I don't want to upset you, but it's very likely that your friend Christopher was among the dead, too. There was a proclamation in the town that all Christian converts must be killed. Now we are in a deadly serious situation, because the *Angrez* will take a terrible revenge on us. And we can forget about any kind of relief or help from them to protect us from the rebel soldiers."

"Because they think Rani Sahiba should have tried to save the prisoners in Jhokun Bagh?"

He shook his head. "Because they'll think she was behind the plot to get them murdered."

"How many died, Bhaiya?"

"The story is, over 60. It was terrible, the slaughter. Men, women, children – all without mercy."

Why did these people, who were not even soldiers, have to be killed? Battles and wars were a fact of life, but why did ordinary people have to die? A fly buzzed near my nose and the thought of clouds of flies swarming over the bloody corpses of the Britishers made my head swim. I swallowed hard and addressed my brother.

"Are you with the Rani now?"

"Yes, I made my decision yesterday. Many of my friends in my regiment have deserted and slipped away quietly to their villages. What else could they do? All the world said that the rule of the British had come to an end, and being God-fearing folk they thought the best refuge was home. Those who have mutinied have been promised twelve rupees a month by the rebel leaders. For this reason alone, many of the 12th Native Infantry regiment and the whole wing of the 14th Bengal Irregular Cavalry have joined the mutineers. But how can I desert the Rani and run back to our village, like a dog with its tail between its legs? And I can't leave you here alone. So, this is where we stay, little brother. At least we have one another. The palace is full of intriguers and spies. You have seen that messages for the Rani never reached her and the message for the British was supposed to be directly from her, but it wasn't; so it's hard to know whom to trust. Some of her courtiers and ministers want her to join the fight against the foreigner, but she must make up her own mind. Now, more than ever before, two honest men are especially welcome."

Even though I was still feeling a little sick, I couldn't help being proud that my brother thought I was a man like him.

While we paced up and down in the broiling sun, talking about what could happen next, we heard a noise behind a small door set into the outer palace wall. Someone was hammering the heavy, iron-studded wood and faintly I could hear shouting from the other side.

"Open, for the love of God! Murder, calamity, death! Open, open!"

My brother fought with the thick iron bolt and at last managed to jerk open the door. Three desperate persons stumbled into the courtyard. One was a woman dressed in a filthy black *burqa*, often worn by Muslim women in the bazaar; she held a small boy by the hand – his shoulder was covered in blood and he was trembling violently. The third was a young man, about my height, bare-chested and wearing just a loincloth and a turban. To my surprise, his grimy face split into a huge grin showing his very white teeth.

"Hanuman! Don't you know me?" The voice, the eyes, the infectious grin! I couldn't quite believe it – this was my old friend Christopher – Saleem, as I knew him.

His words tumbled out. "We managed to escape the slaughter. This is Mrs Mutlow and her son. Her *ayah* smuggled them out of the fort in disguise and I managed to get out as well. We hid in some bushes, then crawled our way here on our bellies. It's terrible in Jhokun Bagh – rivers of blood and corpses everywhere, all being savaged by dogs and vultures!"

Sewak Singh looked round to make sure no one was watching us. "Come on, quick, inside the palace," he whispered. I put my arm around Saleem and led him inside.

When we entered her chambers, the Rani was gazing out of a latticed window. She was deep in thought, with her chin in one hand. Her lady-in-waiting was cooling her with a huge fan, lifting her muslin *dupatta* with the draught.

My brother bowed. "Rani Sahiba, this poor woman needs your help and protection." He indicated

Mrs Mutlow, who had shed her black garment and stood pale and timid between us both.

Rani Lakshmibai's response came as a whiplash. "I can't have her in the palace. It will brand me as being on the English side." But then she saw the pathetic look of the desolate mother. "Who are you? How did you escape the slaughter?"

The English woman replied, "My name is Hannah Mutlow. This is my son, William. I don't know where my husband is, but I pray that he is safe and well. I owe my son's life and mine to our dear *ayah* and to Christopher. Please, Your Highness," she begged, "give us protection and I will tell my countrymen of your mercy to us."

It was a tense few minutes while we watched the Rani's expression soften a little, but to my relief she agreed to let Mrs Mutlow stay in a small, deserted temple in the countryside, about a mile outside the palace. She was ordered to keep her disguise and told that food would be sent to her. Afterwards, I heard that Mrs Mutlow and her child had lived there for a month before being whisked away to Orchha and safety.

Once my brother had escorted Mrs Mutlow and her son through one of the many secret underground passages to her hideaway, it was explained to the other palace staff that Saleem was a relative of a trusted servant of the Rani's and was going to work in the stables. Christopher answered to the name of Saleem once again and the drama that had taken place in the heat of the afternoon remained a closely guarded secret.

"He'll come in very useful as a spy," Sewak Singh told me later. "He knows the layout of the town and cantonment and I think we can rely on him." All kinds of useful information was being gathered for my brother by a few trusted men, but now my friend had been chosen to join that select group. A spy! It sounded so exciting! I'd have done anything to exchange places with Saleem.

I was still camping on the mat in Damodar Rao's bedroom when the Rani sent for me at dawn the next day. She was at her desk in the upper chamber, her maid sprinkling sand on the letter she had just finished. The Rani said, "Go and wake your friend. I need him to take an urgent letter to Jabalpur."

It was Saleem's first mission. No one was to know that he was carrying a message for Captain Erskine, the area Superintendant. I helped him with his disguise. We rubbed grey ash all over his body and he wrapped a raggedy loincloth around his hips to resemble a holy faquir – just like the man I had seen on my way to Orchha with Captain Poole. The Rani's letter was rolled up and inserted inside a bamboo walking stick.

Her letter said that she was very sorry for what had happened to the English in Jhokun Bagh, but that she was not personally responsible for the atrocity. It was important for her to clear her name, because she knew that she would be blamed for the terrible murders. She also asked Erskine to send immediate reinforcements, because now she was extremely vulnerable to attack from her enemies.

It was a very dangerous mission because, had the letter been discovered on his person, Saleem would have paid with his life. The rebel soldiers wouldn't have spared him. And although he was game for the risky adventure, he also had little choice, because he was dependent on the Rani for shelter and protection.

The Rani said, "Wait for a reply. Don't take no for an answer. Tell Erskine what happened in the Jhokun Bagh and how one of my soldiers pretended to have a message of safe conduct from me. This is a great test of your loyalty, Saleem. Jhansi and I are counting on you."

"Take heed – don't get caught," I said as Saleem disappeared into the secret passage that ran underground from the palace to the fort. The hours had flown since his dramatic arrival yesterday and there had been no time to exchange news or to talk to one another. I waited impatiently for him to come back and prayed hard for his safe return.

On 11 June, two days after Saleem's departure, the rebel soldiers robbed the regiment's treasure and looted the cantonment. It was only a mile away from the palace. From the lookout on the roof, I smelled smoke and in the distance saw drifting black plumes in the sky. They were burning the bungalows. Some of the clothes and furniture that had belonged to the English later turned up in the junk shops of the bazaar.

Then a platoon of sowars came galloping up to the palace gates and shouted to be let in. I watched from an upper window as their horses pawed the ground and neighed while the palace guards fetched the Rani. I hurtled downstairs because I wanted to be closer to what was going on.

The Rani made them wait an hour before she came outside, surrounded by her bodyguard. My brother was at her right hand.

"We want 2,000 men, four cannon, half your treasury and six elephants. The Mughal Padshah has asked all the princes of India to contribute to his cause," demanded the leader of the sowars.

"I cannot meet your demands," said the Rani, showing a cool and collected front. I think she had figured out that any womanly weaknesses wouldn't be to her advantage.

"Look, Highness – let me explain something," the soldier said in the tones of an elder and better addressing someone of inferior rank. My blood started to boil. "You are in no position to dictate terms. It won't take us long to join the Larai Rani of Orchha's army and lay siege to your palace. We will set fire to it," he stated baldly, "and we will kill you and your son. You mean nothing to us, unless you support us."

They were blackmailing her. I wondered what she would do now.

Rani Lakshmibai turned on her heels. "You can wait here until I decide what I can afford to give you," she said, before going inside to consult her father and her ministers. I followed, wondering how I could help.

The haggling went on all day. At last the Rani bought temporary peace for herself and Jhansi by giving the sepoys two elephants, 1,000 soldiers from her army, two cannon and gold from the treasury. The soldiers left for Delhi and, after all those days as virtual prisoners, we were able to open our gates and smell the air of freedom again.

Now we waited anxiously for Saleem to come back from Jabalpur. As each day passed, news of what was taking place in the rest of northern India came trickling in. Allahabad, Fatehgarh, Kanpur, Lucknow, Agra – one after the other fell to the sepoys. It truly seemed as though the British were finished, just like the prophecy had said.

Saleem returned safely after handing over the letter from the Rani to Captain Erskine. Saleem brought her Erskine's reply, but there was little in it to comfort her. The Captain had made polite noises about appreciating the Rani's position, but hadn't been able to guarantee the support or reinforcements she wanted and needed.

I had a good view of Rani Lakshmibai's chambers from the stables. Saleem and I had fallen into the habit of meeting there in the evening for a chat; sometimes he would sing verses of ballads he had just composed. The Rani, in turn, could see right across the central courtyard to where her favourite Arab mare was being looked after by Saleem. On the ground right under her windows, which were screened by fretted stonework, was an enormous chessboard, each square in the chessboard being large enough to accommodate a standing person. From her upper storey, the Rani was able to direct her human chess pieces. Having taught her son the rules of the royal game (which I picked up as well) she set him a challenge: she would position her pieces from her upstairs window while she dealt with state papers, and Damodar Rao would be her opponent on the ground.

He was a smart little player, or maybe the Rani was indulging him, because this evening she was surrounded by knight, king, rook and bishop. The prince's dimple deepened with pleasure as he realized that he was about to checkmate his mother. Her laughter rang down from the upper storey.

"Damodar Rao, look, your mother is surrounded by enemies! The king is the English Raj, the knight is the Rani of Orchha, the rook could be the rich landowners – the Thakurs – and the bishop is just one of several states that hate me."

The little prince pulled out a toy pistol, which was an exact replica of the real thing. Pointing it at the palace servants who represented the chess pieces, he shouted, "Bang, bang, bang! Killed you all. Fall down, down, down! Ayee, now you can win if you like!"

All the courtiers and maidservants clapped and cheered politely, but I could sense their unease. The game had brought it home to us all that our kingdom of Jhansi was in reality friendless and alone. Rani Lakshmibai was very aware of our situation and she tried her best to assure the British that she was not part of the mutiny so they would protect her, but they were in no mood to believe her letters of loyalty.

Saleem carried all the Rani's personal correspondence wherever he was sent – to some of the princes who could be called her allies and several more times to Captain Erskine. But Saleem's other job was to snoop around Jhansi town bazaar to pick up titbits of information that might possibly be valuable. He enjoyed wearing different disguises – faquir, toyseller or ballad singer. He would darken the fuzz on his upper lip to look older and, in my eyes, he always looked the part.

One evening in early July, Damodar Rao was being fussed over by his maids because he'd eaten too many mangoes for lunch, so I had a free evening. Saleem and I met at the stable as usual. I said, in what I thought was a casual way, "I am so jealous of you. Being a nursemaid to the prince isn't much fun. I'd give anything to go on one of your adventures."

Saleem looked hard at me. "You hate your job, don't you? Why don't you come with me tonight? I was thinking of going as a wandering ballad singer – you could accompany me on castanets."

"Well, why not?" I replied with a rush of

excitement. We had much merriment dressing up as Rajput gypsies, who are traditionally singers and musicians. We each wore a huge, red turban and borrowed embroidered waistcoats from the palace gardeners. I also "borrowed" the small brass castanets – which were used during prayers – from the palace temple when the priest wasn't looking.

I'd often seen Saleem's heels disappearing into the secret underground tunnel that led from the stables to Jhansi Fort. This time, I followed right behind as he led the way with a candle stump in his hand. The tunnel stank of bat droppings. As we walked, I remembered that evening two months back in Orchha. I wondered if Captain Poole had managed to save himself. There were stories circulating of English fugitives who were hiding in safe places in the countryside and being sheltered by villagers. Others were not so lucky and were hunted down and killed by rebel soldiers. I also wondered about the fate of Mrs Mutlow and her small son. Saleem didn't talk about her, but I knew that his sister, Maria, hadn't been heard of since the Jhokun Bagh massacre.

Saleem padded along, bent half-double, until he suddenly halted. I peered over him to see a pair of luminous, amber lights, and clutched his shoulder.

"Don't worry," he laughed, "It's only a cat after the rats."

"Rats!" A small scream emerged from my throat.

"Ssh. Keep your voice down. Good thing I didn't warn you about the cobra I saw slithering away…" I gave him a shove.

"Come on, Hanuman, this isn't a kid's game. We're spies. Stop twittering like a parakeet."

Our destination was the bazaar in the middle of the town. Jhansi Fort, inside which the English had sheltered for three days in June, was built on a rocky promontory. Its walls were massive blocks of red granite – 20-feet thick and 30-feet high – and the tunnel ended just under them, concealed by a trapdoor hidden under a prickly thorn bush. We climbed out, dusted off the cobwebs and walked boldly up one of the many lanes that led to the interior of old Jhansi.

When we reached the bazaar, oil lamps were smoking outside the shops, which were piled high with all kinds of goods – mounds of guavas, mangoes, custard apples and bright green, orange, yellow and purple vegetables. Sticky sweets bubbled in big black pans and there was a delicious smell of frying *bhajis*. Goldsmiths weighed their precious metal on tiny scales, and blacksmiths stoked their roaring fires as they fashioned the country muskets, lances and arrows for which the town was famous. Crowds of strollers and window-shoppers paused to gather in groups and we overheard snatches of news about the disturbances that were erupting all over the northern provinces. Knots of stragglers from the Bengal Army gathered to plan their next move. After the peaceful order of the palace, it was full of fun and interest, like a country fair.

Saleem chose his site with care. Stationing himself near a group of soldiers, he struck a pose, hand on hip and chin raised. Then he launched into a ballad about a princess and a poor woodcutter. His bold voice cut through the babble and people stopped to listen. I had my instructions to click the castanets in any way I saw fit, but also to listen out for stray bits of news and gossip in the crowd. It consisted of Brahmin priests, farmers, soldiers and city dandies with sprigs of jasmine behind one ear and diamond buttons in their shirts. Then I noticed two men standing on the edge of the crowd. They weren't in uniform, but they had a military bearing and sported fierce handlebar moustaches. They were listening attentively to Saleem's singing. As he launched into a new verse with a flourish of his arm, two brawny fellows went up to these men and tried to knock them down. An uproar broke out as the four men rolled around in the dust. Then, all at once, the disturbance erupted into a much bigger, general fight among the rest of the crowd. Saleem's voice died away.

"Just watch and listen and don't say a word," whispered Saleem to me.

Then the brawny men shouted in ringing tones, "Rissaldars Kalu Khan and Ahmed Husain, we arrest you in the name of the Governor General for conspiring to overthrow the British Raj in Jhansi!"

"Traitors!" retorted the moustachioed men fiercely. One spat in the face of his assailant. "You'll burn in hell for claiming a reward from the foreigner! Shame on you!"

"Shame!" roared the crowd who were on the side of the victims. The situation quickly became very ugly, as people started kicking and punching the brawny men, who seemed to be agents of the British.

"Kill them!" they shouted. "Lynch the cowards!"

The crowd was ready to tear the British agents to pieces, and Saleem and I hopped into a doorway where we could watch safely. My friend observed, "Jhansi townspeople are completely with the rebel soldiers."

Minutes later the Jhansi jailer arrived and hustled away the British agents. We heard later that the jailer had stabbed them to death.

Afterwards, while we sat at a sherbet stall, we learned that the first two men were local heroes and ringleaders of the Jhansi mutiny, with a price of 1,000 rupees on each of their heads. The stallholder and his customers told us that they were trying to recruit runaway soldiers to their cause. They promised that the old Mughal king in Delhi would pay them double their army salary.

"Come, Hanuman." Saleem got up to leave. "We've learned enough for one night. The Rani must be told that the people of Jhansi will never allow her to hide under the protection of the British." On our return to the palace, we thought that the news we carried was important enough to wake the Rani from her sleep, even though it was four in the morning.

"Want to see a picture of the Devil, of *Shaitan*?" Saleem had been to the Jhansi bazaar on another errand. He unfurled a poster. An evil-looking man with a cruel rubbery mouth leered from it.

> WANTED DEAD OR ALIVE.
> NANA SAHIB – THE MOST WANTED MAN
> IN INDIA.
> 100,000 RUPEES FOR HIS CAPTURE

"They're all over the bazaars of every town in the district. My latest information is that Nana Sahib and Tantia Topey are on their way to these parts."

"What are they going to do?" I asked Saleem. Nathu, who was another member of my brother's team of spies, was with us in the stables that evening. Several years older than either of us, he was a wily and experienced veteran in the business of espionage.

"Are you the village idiot, Hanuman?" Nathu was astonished by my ignorance. "When the Peshwa died he left Nana Sahib his entire and enormous fortune, but the British had already annexed his kingdom, so he was on a pretty substantial pension as well. A *very* substantial pension, I tell you. Well, the *Angrez* refused to carry the pension over to Nana Sahib. He was hopping mad! He did everything – threatened the English, sent his secretary Azimullah to the *Inglistan* Queen Victoria to petition her. Huh, all that fool Azimullah accomplished was to get betrothed to several white women across the Black Water. Back he came – empty-handed – but I heard that he stopped in Russia, in the Crimea, where the British were fighting a very big war. Nana Sahib discovered that our white rulers are not invincible – they lost thousands of men in that war. This made him even bolder. He is a cunning old fox. Last month, he promised safe conduct to hundreds of British residents of Kanpur, but had them all butchered on the banks of the Ganges. And this is the reason he is the British Enemy Number One."

"Would you betray him to the British for the reward?" I asked.

"Maybe," Nathu said, pulling at his hubble-bubble pipe. "He's not from these parts, so I don't owe him anything. Now, I would do anything for our Rani, but foreigners are another matter."

"And Tantia Topey?"

"A great fighter. He dashes into battle, and then, when everyone is knocking each other's heads together, Tantia gallops off to re-group. But let me tell you, out of them all our Rani is the one with most sense and courage." He picked up the bazaar poster. "Ugh. What a villainous face!"

"Tch, he doesn't really look like that," Saleem

reproved. "That's *their* idea of him – how the British want others to see him."

I remarked, "He did have a lot of innocent women and children killed."

"And the British are angels from heaven, are they? Every day, we hear that they are burning villages, stringing up sepoys like jackals and firing them from cannon as live ammunition." Saleem leaned forward, his eyes dark with foreboding. "This is the lull before the storm. We're in for difficult times, brothers. Fighting is on its way, from Orchha, from the Thakurs and from the British. And the ones I fear most are the British."

"Have you heard the latest news about the Larai Rani of Orchha? I picked it up on the road to Hamirpur." Nathu gurgled into his hubble-bubble pipe. "She's sheltering a group of English fugitives – men, women and children, or rather her son's Brahmin tutor is. So Orchha's the unquestionable ally of the British and the tutor's just been richly rewarded with two embroidered Kashmiri shawls, a very handsome sabre, a gold-lined cloak and a pouch of 50 gold sovereigns. I wouldn't say no if they offered me that!"

August 1857

During August of that year, I wasn't sleeping well. At three in the morning, I'd be suddenly awake and then I'd lie there until dawn, thinking of our village and the *kharif* crop. How was Father going to manage without my help? Then, one morning as I lay with my worries shunting back and forth, an idea alighted like a moth and helped me to relax and at last drift off... I had the solution to the monkey problem that had plagued us for the last two years! This is what we would do – plant tall cactus hedges around the fields and chop down any overhanging branches that allowed the creatures to jump down on our chickpeas and plunder us. But then I'd have to find a way for us to get to the crops, without allowing those pests in as well... I hadn't given my family much thought until now, but thinking of our fields brought a great gnawing homesickness over me. I imagined that I could smell my mother's cooking. The palace food had been great to begin with, but it was too rich for my stomach.

My mouth felt parched, so I got up to fetch a drink

of water, stumbling in the darkness to the well in the adjoining courtyard. It was so early, just a shade short of night, that the noise and activity coming from that section of the palace alerted me to something unusual. What was my brother doing at this hour? I caught a glimpse of him hurrying towards the stables, so I followed. His horse was saddled and ready, along with a dozen sowars, each with a gun strapped to his saddle.

"Father has sent an urgent message for me to return and help him out for a few days. Our neighbouring Thakur in the next village has invaded Digna and carried off herds and grain. Just imagine, old Despat Singh has become a bandit in his old age! He demanded protection money from Father against the real bandits that are roaming all over the countryside. I've warned the Rani that the law and order situation is getting out of hand. The countryside is all stirred up with talk of war and anarchy and everyone seems to be taking the law into their own hands. Rani Sahiba has asked me to help the generals reorganize the army when I get back." With that, he turned his horse and was on his way.

"Let me come." My shout followed after him, but he had gone.

Two days later Sewak Singh was back, having succeeded in charging Despat Singh's village and knocking down its mud walls. "Sometimes attack is the best form of defence," he told me. "Despat won't bully our family any more." In his saddlebag, he carried presents for Saleem and me: cotton shirts, home-made pickle and a bottle of hair oil from my mother.

I rubbed some of the oil into my hair. "What'll you do when we can go back home again?" I asked Saleem.

"One, pay off our debts with my earnings. Two, try and re-join the Army – this time as a sowar. Let's join up together!"

Sewak Singh had barely returned from his mission, when news came that the Orchha Army was invading some of the outlying villages that belonged to Jhansi.

The niggling enmity between Jhansi and Orchha had suddenly turned deadly serious. September arrived and with it war.

Damodar Rao insisted on being dressed in his miniature army uniform. Sword clanking at his side and a pistol in each hand, he marched to the stables to "oversee" his mother's mare being made ready for the campaign. I was ordered to keep six paces behind him, and had to stop myself snorting with laughter at his childish, self-important swagger.

There were seven generals, Hindu and Muslim, in the Rani's army, but she always headed it herself. I had never seen her leave for battle with her horsemen and foot soldiers behind her and it was a wonderful sight indeed. She wore a black sari with gold edging, looped between her legs so she could ride astride, and a metal breastplate and a bandana around her head, and carried a sword and shield. Her face was a mask of steely determination. My heart swelled with admiration for her. My brother had been promoted to become the head of the cavalry, and the prince and I waited by the gates to wave them off, standing there until long after the vanguard was hidden by a cloud of white dust.

Saleem, Nathu and the other spies were like vultures, foraging for news on the outskirts of the action. They learned that the Orchha commander had galloped all the way to Gwalior and asked for a hearing with the British representative. He convinced him that the Rani of Jhansi had sanctioned the Jhokun Bagh massacre and was on the side of the rebel soldiers. That's when the English started calling her the Jezebel of India.

The name meant nothing to me, but Saleem had been taught the Christian's holy book and said that Jezebel was a *churail* – a very evil woman.

After two days of fighting, the Jhansi Army retreated into Jhansi Fort. The enemy kept up a steady cannonade, but they couldn't breach the defence. The prince and I watched from the palace rooftop as our soldiers drove off the Orchha men with continuous gunfire and our heavy guns. Sewak Singh managed to leave the fort by a gate at the back and swept round with a company to attack the enemy on its right flank, during which we saw dozens of Orchha soldiers being mown down.

When the worst of the fighting was over, the Rani came back to the palace through one of the secret tunnels that ran underneath the fort. After that, it took several more weeks for the enemy to concede defeat, but we all knew that they were hovering in the wings, waiting for another chance to attack Jhansi.

Events around us speeded up to such an extent that Saleem was busy travelling most of the time and was hardly ever in Jhansi. He'd come for two or three days and disappear for a week. Another syce was appointed to look after the Rani's mare. Letters and messages of reassurance flew between the Rani and her allies, the Raja of Banpur and Nawabs of Banda and Shahgarh.

The rains had only just petered out at the beginning of September and, though it was still very hot, the sun wasn't at its most lancing. It was getting to be almost pleasant to sit outside after it had set.

"It's not fun and games any more, Hanuman," Saleem yawned, rubbing his eyes, as we squatted over his clay stove. He looked listless and his eyes were shadowed with dark circles. A pot of *dal* was simmering for our supper. I ate with him whenever I got the chance because his *chapattis* and *dal* tasted like they did in our village, deliciously smoky from the wood. We scooped up morsels of pickle and *dal* as we exchanged news.

"See," he bared his arm and pointed at a wound. "That was given by an Orchhan sepoy who caught me straying on their side of the Betwa River. I had to run like the wind into the jungle, climb a *neem* tree and stay put for three hours."

He pooh-poohed my concern that he should get his arm bandaged. "It's only a scratch," he said dismissively.

"What news did you pick up for the Rani?"

My question made him liven up a little. "Not only for the Rani but her seven generals as well! The most important is bad news. Delhi has been recaptured by the British after very bloody fighting and a hard siege."

"The Mughal emperor?"

"Locked up again in the tomb of his ancestor Humayun, on the outskirts of the capital. A Captain Hodson arrested the Mughal emperor's two younger sons and shot them in cold blood in front of their courtiers. The dog! Delhi people are seething with anger, but are also very frightened because the British and their loyal sepoys went on a rampage of looting – streets of shops and houses were destroyed in Chandni Chowk near the Jama Masjid. It's our turn next – the British want the Rani and they want revenge for what happened in Jhokun Bagh…"

We'd barely washed our fingers and rinsed out our mouths when a page came rushing into our sanctuary, panting and out of breath. "Hanuman Singh, come quickly. The Rani Sahiba wants you now. The *Haldi Kunku puja* is beginning and she wants you to look after Damodar Rao."

Our Rani was a very religious lady. She went to her temple every day, and was always arranging special prayers and *pujas*. I think this is why the people of Jhansi didn't criticize her for wearing men's clothes and riding a horse. They respected her very much. The Rani had arranged this *Haldi Kunku* ceremony in honour of the goddess Lakshmi and her *durbar* room was decorated all over with flowers. Sticks of incense perfumed the air. In the centre of the room was a statue of Lakshmi, after whom our Rani was named, smothered with garlands of jasmine and marigold. A bare-chested priest circled the statue with a tray of coconut, rice and a small oil-fed light, while the Rani acknowledged the greetings of townspeople who had come to take part in the ceremony with her. She was wearing a white, silk sari with her necklace of large pearls and looked very beautiful. There was something so noble and solemn about her that I held my breath with awe. She beckoned to me.

"Hanuman Singh, I have some special work for you. Come into my chamber after the ceremony is over. Your brother and I want you to undertake a mission for us."

I had to wait three hours before I found out what the mission was, but some instinct told me that it did not involve rigging up jumping ropes for the prince. I felt in my bones that I was going to be asked to do something very important.

The Rani was standing by her window, the one that looked out over the city walls. My brother stood respectfully near the door. The chamber was in darkness, but an oil lamp lit up the corner where she stood. A heap of jasmine garlands lay tossed on the floor and a maid listlessly swung a heavy fan to create some moving air.

The Rani asked me to sit on the floor near her. With barely suppressed excitement, she told me that Nana Sahib and Tantia Topey had been sighted in the area near Digna village. "I am giving you a huge responsibility. I want you to seek them out and invite them to join my alliance against the British! The festival of *Bhai-dooj* is next week, so you have a perfectly legitimate reason to go home to celebrate. No one in the palace knows the country around Digna like you, and it's likely that Nana Sahib will visit the travelling fair in Digna to recruit soldiers to their cause. If you are careful, none of our enemies will suspect that you've sown the seeds of a future alliance between the Rani of Jhansi and the Maratha leader." My brother nodded his agreement. "If we have a really strong alliance then we have a good chance against the British. We are still hoping they won't march against us, but it's only a small hope. Their ears have been poisoned against Rani Sahiba, so we must make contingency plans."

The Rani added, "The vital thing is that the British, or those who side with them, do not get wind of this proposed alliance between Nana Sahib and Jhansi, so you must move lightly and not be noticed. Not a breath of this will be heard outside my room. I don't trust anyone."

I swallowed, taken aback at the greatness of her faith in me, completely over the moon at my incredible good fortune. I had only fantasized about such an opportunity; now here was my big chance to prove that I could be as good a spy as Saleem.

Prince Damodar Rao sulked and screamed when I told him I had to go home. "I want to go with you! I hate Sushilabai!" he wailed. Sushilabai was his nurse. "Why do you have to go? Why doesn't your sister come here?"

"Prince, brothers have to go to their sister's house for *Bhai-dooj* to get their blessing. Saleem will come and tell you stories while I'm away."

But the prince held his breath and kept up his high-pitched screaming until his eyes started to pop. "I hate you! I'm going to shoot you till your liver is pulp!"

I felt like giving him a good thrashing for the spoiled puppy that he was, but asked instead if he wanted to hear a story about *Bhai-dooj*. He nodded, and stopped his tantrum. He settled down to listen because one thing he couldn't resist was a story.

"Once upon a time, a brother and sister loved each other very much." I stretched my arms as wide as I could. "When the festival of *Bhai-dooj* arrived, the brother travelled to his sister's married home to get his blessing from her. On the way to her village, he was attacked by tigers who wanted to gobble him up. 'Please, oh, please let me go to my sister, and on my way home you can eat me if you wish,' he said.

78

"Next, he came across snakes and scorpions who wanted to bite him, so he asked them to postpone that pleasure until he was on his way back home.

"After that, he had to cross the flooded Ganges, which threatened to drown him. 'Wait until I return,' he begged the river.

"At last, he reached his sister's house and she was so overjoyed to see him that she hugged him and hugged him till he could hardly breathe! She put a paste of sandalwood and rice on his forehead as a blessing, a sweet in his mouth and made him sit down, while she prepared a meal for his journey back home. But something terrible happened – as she was grinding the flour for his *chappatis*, a poisonous snake fell into the grindstone without her noticing.

"She wrapped up the picnic meal and said goodbye to her brother. He set off with a terrible dread in his heart. Then the sister fed her little dog the remains of the *chapatti* dough, and what do you know? The dog fell down and died!"

The prince was lying comfortably on a cushion, sucking his thumb and listening attentively. I continued my story.

"Then, the sister cried, 'My poor brother!' and prayed to all the gods that they would stop him before he ate any of her food. She started to run as fast as she could and she finally caught up with him. 'Oh, brother, I am so happy that I've stopped you from dying a certain death. Now I will travel back to your home with you,' she said.

"When they reached the Ganges, the river reminded him of what was going to happen to him, but the sister prayed to the holy river and it spared her brother. Then, when they came upon the snakes and scorpions, she fed them some milk and they let her brother go. Then she spoke so sweetly to the tigers that they agreed to spare her brother. And so she accompanied her brother safely home.

"Now, Your Highness, my sister has to give three blessings when I go back. One for you, one for Sewak Singh and one for me! And these blessings will protect us three for the rest of the year."

"But I'm not her brother," the prince protested.

"No, but she can adopt you as her brother. That's the custom in our village."

"Bring me back a present from the village fair," the prince cried petulantly. I promised that I would.

It was 10 October, and all the way home I kept meeting bullock carts belonging to the Banjara tribe, who were travelling to set up the annual fair held near our village.

Everyone was overjoyed to see me home again and Saleem's mother, Aminabai, couldn't get enough news of her son, whom she had thought was lost to her for ever. She rejoiced, "And you say that he still calls himself by his given name? He is still my Saleem? Allah be praised!"

My little sister jumped up and down at the prospect of going to the fair with me.

"Will you buy me blue glass bangles, Bhaiya?"

"Why not red?"

"All the other girls are wearing blue."

"I'll buy you a ribbon for your hair as well," I promised her. The Rani had given me five gold *mohurs*, so I had plenty of money to share with my family.

Of course, I didn't say a word to Father about the real reason for my visit home, but next day when my sister and I walked hand-in-hand to the fairground that was all I could think about. Our first stop was the bangle-seller's stall. Then, when my sister's little forearm was satisfyingly covered in shiny, blue glass, we made our way to the fairground rides.

It was the perfect occasion for anonymous meetings and exchanges. Knots of people, whom I had never before seen in our area, stood around. There were travelling merchants, buyers and sellers. Men with beards and turbans from the far North, magic-lantern men, toysellers with their bamboo contraptions hung with every trinket and bauble under the sun, fire-eaters, gypsies with performing bears and dancing monkeys. The noise and dust and excitement created a screen of confusion that would have masked a hundred undercover transactions.

My sister nagged me endlessly about going on the merry-go-round, but then her attention was distracted by a dusty, brown mountain bear. It was being twirled round and round in a clumsy kind of dance. Its keeper was a Kashmiri, who barked orders at the bear. "Lie down, *bhalloo*. Die for the emperor! Stand up again." And so on. My sister was entranced, but I let my eyes rake through the bystanders, hoping to see something of a little more interest. Saleem had taught me to be alert to people on the edge of crowds, to people hiding in shadows and sheltering behind camels. I saw nothing unusual at all, until my roving eye lit upon three Muslim women huddled together near the sugarcane-juice stall. They were accompanied by a man whose smoothshaven cheeks and clothes made me think he couldn't be a Muslim. To my eyes there was something a little too squat about him, and gold rings dangled from both ears.

"Stay here," I hissed to my sister. "Don't move until I come back." Then I casually edged my way towards the group of four, trying not to be conspicuous, just as Saleem had taught me. The three women were shrouded in black *burqas* with eye-holes made of net, so it was impossible to see their faces. But something happened to confirm my initial suspicions about the group. A wasp detached itself from the swarm gathering round the sticks of sugarcane, and circled around the women, before alighting on the eyehole of one of their *burqas*. She brought out her hand from under her black gown and flicked at the insect. *But it was a man's hand – large and powerful, with hairs growing right down to the wrist!*

Only the threat of real danger would make three men dress up as women. My instinct told me that I had located my prey. Now I had to be extremely cautious, in case a spy from the Orchha camp, who would doubtless know of my Jhansi connection, saw me talking directly to the women. I had to approach the quartet in an indirect way, preferably without speaking. There was a *kikar* tree fairly close to where they sat, but I couldn't climb it without drawing attention to myself. A bullock cart stood nearby, so I managed to circle behind the "women" and wriggle myself under the cart.

"I've managed to recruit 200 from this area and have been promised another 600," the male escort growled in a low voice.

"The best thing is to get the Gwalior contingent to desert Maharajah Scindia, who is totally at one with the British. I'll have to start working on that. We need thousands of soldiers, not hundreds." This deep voice came from one of the "ladies".

A third added, "If only we had the allegiance of the Rani of Jhansi – she has some troops and heavy guns, as well as money in her treasury."

The fourth said, "Not only that but she is a formidable warrior. I should know – we had fencing lessons together as children." This last speaker could be none other than Nana Sahib. So he was in these parts to recruit soldiers for his army!

How was I to get their attention without being noticed by anyone else? I was afraid that any minute now they would move off and I would lose sight of them. Crawling out from under the cart, I looked frantically around me. In a quieter corner of the fairground, I spotted a letter writer, with his portable desk, paper and quill pens, taking dictation from a farmer. Hurrying over to him, I held out two rupees. "A piece of paper and the use of your pen!" Snatching up the writing material before he could protest, I scribbled a note: "Revered Sirs, I have some important information from the lady you have been discussing. Meet me near the fortune-telling parrot."

But when I traced my steps back to the sugarcane man, the four had disappeared!

I was in a frenzy of disappointment. So near and yet so far! Where could they be? I checked that my sister was all right. "Stay right here," I told her, and ran towards where the camels and horses were tethered. My prey had just climbed into their camel cart and were about to head off. I went up to the camel driver and, making sure that no one was looking, handed him my note. "For your master," I said and wandered back to the fair, casually, as though I didn't have a care in the world. I squatted, to make myself less conspicuous, in the shade of an awning next to where the fortune-telling parrot was pecking at cards. And I waited.

In a little while, the round-faced man with the gold earrings appeared and joined me.

"Well, young fellow, what do you want? Hurry now, I have no time to waste." His voice was gruff.

"The lady is interested in an alliance."

"She is wooing the British. My masters have no patience with two-timers."

"She will give up on the white men if you join her."

"I'll tell them to keep it in mind. She can send us word when she is completely sure of her loyalty." He turned on his heels, but changed his mind and came back to me. Looking around to make sure that he wasn't being followed, he said rapidly, "Tell your Rani that the British are starting to march this way. It will be a massive army under General Rose. She hasn't got much time to decide…" He glanced around him, before strolling back to his camel cart and his "harem".

My mission was accomplished. I had made contact and could take a message back to the palace. I went to join my sister and we continued to do our round of the fair, but I found that my heart was beating faster than normal. Now, all I wanted was to get back to Jhansi as soon as possible.

My mission had taken just three days and I returned to Jhansi just in time for *Diwali*, though my sister made such a fuss that I nearly stayed at home for the festival. Before, I had been so homesick that I had dreamed of going back to Digna. Now, less than a week after returning to my family, I couldn't wait to get back to the palace. What would happen now? Would the Rani find forgiveness with the British? Would they believe her word and protect her from the anger of the rebel soldiers and her neighbouring enemies? Or would she be forced to join up with Nana Sahib and Tantia Topey in an all-out stand against the foreign power? It seemed to me that the situation in Jhansi hung in the balance – the Rani was poised and waiting to see how best to secure her kingdom for herself and Damodar Rao.

As I walked up the road to the palace, in the blue and purple dusk of early winter, I caught my breath at the beautiful sight of thousands of tiny flames that flickered like glow-worms from every wall and parapet. The court musicians were playing softly in the background. Not even an inch of darkness was permitted as this might have turned away Lakshmi, the goddess of prosperity. The *Diwali* atmosphere inside the palace was so peaceful that it was hard to imagine that, behind the scenes, the Rani's advisers, were quarrelling about what course of action she should take. Saleem's arm hadn't healed either. An infection from his wound had spread to his hand and he lay in bed with a fever, glassy-eyed and listless. He was so ill that the story of my encounter with Nana Sahib hardly stirred more than polite interest.

However, my brother congratulated me on my successful trip. He complained, "I'm fed up with all the bickering between Moro Pant and the generals. They keep confusing the Rani with contradictory advice. Half say that she should go with the British." He mimicked one of the generals. "'The English are masters – no one can stand up to them. They are coming with more men and guns than we can deal with.' The other half want her to fight them. And your news that Nana Sahib and Tantia Topey will only pledge support after she's come off the fence makes it more complicated." Sighing deeply he continued. "Being the Rani's close adviser on military matters is exhausting. So, with one of my best spies laid up sick, you'll have to work directly under me. Rani Sahiba has agreed to release you from domestic duties."

I was speechless, absolutely thrilled at this new turn

of events. No more nursemaid duties, no more flattering a spoiled prince!

He put his arm around me. "Yes, you've done well, little brother. But now it's essential that you take your orders from me and no one else. Your first task is to travel to Indore and Gwalior to find out what the British are planning. Who is their commander? How many men and guns do they have? And so on. Most importantly, I need to know when they intend marching to Jhansi. You won't be able to go alone, so Nathu will accompany you."

This was a much bigger job than the one I'd just finished. A tiny doubt surfaced about my abilities as a spy. Maybe my previous success had been a fluke. Maybe Saleem could help me and give me some tips. I would pick his brains as soon as he was better.

A few days later, Saleem was up to sitting in bed, but still needed help in going to the bathroom. He was getting better with the traditional *Unani* treatment of poultices and herbs, but his diet of boiled vegetables and rice was beginning to bore him. Until a few days back, he'd hardly been able to swallow anything.

I sat on the end of the bed and explained my nervousness and great lack of confidence. "You have to help me, Saleem. How will I get this information about troop movements? Who should I talk to? That kind of news doesn't get hung out to dry on a laundry line." Suddenly I felt as if I was floundering in monsoon mud.

"Think, Hanuman," said Saleem. "Where do soldiers hang about? Who is likely to possess this kind of information?"

"They live in cantonments, but surely only the British officers will get news of troop movements directly."

Saleem demanded, "Who else?"

"The English Governor General's representative in Indore. Sewak Singh told me his name is Himmat Singh or something like it."

Saleem laughed out aloud, and that was good to hear. "No, donkey. *Hamilton*. I think the best thing is for you and Nathu to find employment in Sir Robert Hamilton's bungalow. After all, you've been a nanny to Damodar Rao so you could—"

I reached out with my fists, pretending to box him. "Shut your mouth. Enough!"

"Seriously though, get a job in the kitchens helping the cook and you'll pick up all sorts of useful news."

"I can't do washing-up. I'm a Rajput," I protested.

But when I met with my brother and Nathu to discuss our plans, they both agreed that Saleem's idea of joining Hamilton's household was the simplest and most straightforward one. Nathu was to teach me some tricks of the trade, while Saleem would drill me in English expressions.

He tested me every day till I left for Indore, and I began to recognize *Good morning, memsahib, water, at once, yes sir, no master* and other stupid English words of command.

Saleem also told me that soon it would be the English people's big festival, their *Burra Din*. "It's called Christmas," he said, "and you must say 'Happy Christmas!' to the Sahib and Memsahib."

And so, one chilly December morning Nathu and I set off, hoping to find rides all the way to Indore, which lay a good distance to the south-west of Jhansi. They say that fortune favours the brave, and I am sure it's true. Within a day of arriving in Indore, through Nathu's contacts in the bazaar, we found ourselves employed as washer-uppers in the kitchens of Sir Robert Hamilton's spacious bungalow. Our boss was a mean, alcoholic, Bengali cook who had no hesitation in cuffing me around the ears if I so much as looked like I might voice a thought.

I had never before seen the inside of an English person's house and I was amazed and horrified at the difference in our way of living. "They eat with metal knives and forks! How can food taste of anything?" I exclaimed to Nathu.

"Even worse, they bath in a tub – ugh! All that dirty water slopping around them." Instead, we washed ourselves all over in running water that was sluiced over us from a pump or by emptying a beaker dipped into a bucket of water.

Neither could I understand how the Memsahib could eat her meals with the Sahib. In our home, my mother and sister always served the menfolk first, before eating by themselves in the kitchen. And the kitchen! So many pots and pans, plates and cups, tureens and trays, teapots and coffee-pots!

It was completely fascinating to me, but I was there to do a job of work and there was no shortage of gossip that came filtering down to the kitchen. I made secret notes of anything that might be worth telling back home. It was so cold now that my fingers were always numb from being in water most of the day and half the night. How these people used up crockery and cutlery!

A great bustle of activity connected to their *Burra Din* now began. One day the Burra Sahib, Sir Robert Hamilton, came storming into the kitchen, shouting his head off.

"Who cut down my tree? The big evergreen I planted by the carriage drive!"

For some reason, he thrust his fleshy, red face into mine. His pale blue eyes were bulging out of their sockets. "Well, boy, answer me. Was it you? Where's that damned gardener?" And out he stormed again, like a hurricane.

The Bengali cook chuckled. "Oho, the big Sahib is

tippled! Too much punch and too much rum in the punch."

"Why is he so worried about a tree?" I wondered aloud.

"Because these white people worship that sort of tree on their *Burra Din*. So he thinks the gardener has cut it down to sell to other white folk. He wants to worship his own tree."

I shook my head. Tree worship was something that the primitive tribal people did in the depths of the jungle.

Meanwhile, the Memsahib had started visiting the kitchen every day to supervise the preparations for her "Christmas cake" and "plum pudding". She stood over the cook while he cut up nuts and dried fruit and weighed the butter and flour. I think she did not want him to steal her festive ingredients.

Nathu and I did our best to hang around, listening at doors and running errands for the other more senior servants, in the hope of hearing some interesting military news. One evening we heard a lot of shouting and banging at the front door. A lame black horse was being led round to the back by one of the *syces* while a British cavalry officer, covered in white dust, clamoured to be allowed into the house.

I found an excuse to carry a jug and basin of water to the dining-room, where I hoped to eavesdrop on something of interest. But the doors to the sitting room were firmly closed and I couldn't make out anything other than the murmur of voices. I nearly jumped out of my skin when the door was suddenly flung open and the irate face of our Sahib looked in my direction.

"What the devil are you doing here? Get back to where you belong!" he roared.

On 20 December our Bengali torturer said casually, "Lot of guests coming for *Burra Din*. Lot of tips, if you boys are good."

"Who is coming, sir?" I dared to ask. The cook must have had a few drinks, so he was unusually talkative. "Central Field Force officers commanded by General Hugh Rose from Bombay. He is leading 4,500 infantry, cavalry and artillery. They won't stay long," mused the cook. "They are heading east to Jhansi and Bundelkhand to punish that bad woman."

I wished that I could knock down the disgusting little toady. All these servants of white people thought no end of themselves and had adopted their masters' politics and prejudices.

But now I didn't have to spend another day with this breed. Nathu and I had the information we had come for. It had been handed to us on a large, china serving dish! We didn't need to wait. Without any regrets, we threw our dishcloths away and deserted our jobs. That very night we were on our way back to Jhansi.

Only two weeks later General Rose's army was making its triumphant way through Bundelkhand. At the same time, soldiers belonging to the armies of Rajas who were enemies of the British started to desert their armies. Rose's army was drawing closer and closer to Jhansi. We all waited to see which side of the fence the Rani would choose…

Have you noticed the stillness before a storm shows its frightening power? The lull, not so different from a lullaby in sound, which almost hypnotizes you into thinking that nothing much can happen? That's what those early spring months were like. But we all knew the storm was about to break, and the stillness concealed something more sinister. Sewak Singh was busy recruiting soldiers – raw men from the countryside, who needed discipline and drilling, and other more experienced men, who had deserted Orchha and other states to follow the example of the rebel sepoys and fight the British. The Rani drilled her own women. Every afternoon, she watched them like a hawk as they were taken through their paces by a shrill-voiced woman Rissaldar, whose neck muscles bulged when she screamed, "*Righ-yat turrn!*"

We respected the Rani because she could fight like a man and she knew about wars. Sewak Singh told me that while I was in Indore he had held her armour for her when she crossed swords with a bandit chief called

Sagar Singh. This bandit had defied her authority and said that he wasn't going to pay his taxes, so she rode to his village and challenged him to a duel. My brother told me that her swordplay was brilliant, better than any man's. Sagar Singh was defeated and he threw down his weapon, swearing life-long loyalty to Rani Lakshmibai. But then we all felt that way about her.

I was asked to carry one last letter for the Rani. It was meant for General Rose, who by now had reached Talbehat, about 25 miles away, and taken control of it. His aim was to break the fragile alliance of the princes who were friendly with our Rani.

"This is my very last appeal to the British," said the Rani to my brother. "In the end, I know I can't hold out against them, but I want to try and persuade them that I am still open to being their ally. From what I've heard, they are already putting up my gallows. This letter explains again what was really going on during Jhokun Bagh – chaos and confusion. I was being held to ransom! Do you remember how the sepoys threatened to kill me and my son? Why can't the British understand my position?"

The letter was written in complete secrecy in the Rani's inner chamber and I had to conceal my mission from everyone – not even Saleem knew that I had left the palace. I was instructed to walk to the north side of Jhansi town and hire a pony cart from a one-eyed Muslim called Abbas Mian. In my palm was the gold piece to pay him, and the letter was hidden in the inner sole of my right shoe.

The moon was high so I kept to the shadows, more than once turning to look over my shoulder. Once, I was sure that I saw a dark shape flitting from one side of the lane to the other; I froze in my tracks and watched, but nothing more happened.

Some shops in the bazaar were open late and so were the drinking dens in the heart of the city. I was nearly at Abbas Mian's place now, and I turned into a narrow lane overhung with balconies. All the houses were dark, so I could only see by the light of the moon. I took care not to step into the shallow sewer running in the middle of the pathway. Nobody seemed to be about, and the windows were shuttered up for the night. I had nearly reached Abbas' stables.

It all happened so quickly. One moment I was walking along, the next I was on the ground. Something was pressed against my nose. I was choking – and after that I don't remember anything.

My next memory was that the sun was up. I found

myself being examined by two curious buffaloes. They regarded me amiably, chewing their fodder, and not bothering to move away while they did their business – in fact, I was covered with their dung. Someone must have dumped me in this cowshed. Why had this happened to me? What was that throbbing pain in my head? Why did my shoulder hurt? And then it came back to me. With a yelp, I realized that my shoes had disappeared, and with them the letter that I was supposed to take to Talbehat.

Even though my head was splitting, I knew that I couldn't lie in the cowshed for ever. A wide shaft of brilliant sunshine hit me square in the eyes. Now, as well as the stars in my head, there were motes of dust whirling and thickening my vision, so I could scarcely see beyond my nose.

Groaning with each breath, I dragged myself to a standing position and made myself step outside. I was in the courtyard of a *haveli* – a town house – and the heavy wooden door into the lane outside stood invitingly open with its chain dangling free, left wide open for me to walk away.

By then the sun was well up. Several people looked curiously at me. No wonder – I was covered in sticky, green buffalo dung and I stank. I stumbled along the lane, walking the few remaining yards to my planned destination. But Abbas Mian's door was locked from the inside and no one answered my knocks. Disappointment in my failed mission tasted even worse than the metallic taste of physical pain in my mouth. I turned back and hobbled slowly back to the palace.

Once I got there I passed out. When I regained consciousness, I was stretched out on a bed in the stables, and Saleem was sitting next to me fanning my face.

Before I could say anything, Saleem's eyes widened with surprise and someone entered his room. He jumped up to his feet and bowed. Moro Pant, Rani Lakshmibai's father, was leaning on his ivory-topped cane by my sickbed. He was dressed in his customary white clothes and black pill-box cap. His clear grey eyes met mine.

"Truly, I am sorry that you have suffered, Hanuman. I did not want them to hurt you, only take away the letter meant for the English general." He was embarrassed at having to explain his actions to someone as young and unimportant as myself. But the Rani was known to be very fond of me and dependent on my brother, so I was someone, even when I was nobody, if you see what I mean.

"I owe you an explanation," continued the old gentleman, perching at the end of my bed. "I feel strongly that we must not ally ourselves with the British, and many of the Rani's generals agree with me. The Rani is the queen, but she is a woman after all. We have to fight the British and drive them away. My daughter is a practical person – perhaps a little too practical in this case. She has calculated – wrongly, I feel – that we cannot overcome the British forces; especially as Scindia of Gwalior has strengthened their arm with his own superbly trained men. You know that the French and the English spent many years teaching the Gwalior soldiers their skills. Rani Sahiba says, *were* there an equal chance of winning she would fight, but defeat at the hands of the foreigner will mean the gallows for us all."

Moro Pant's old eyes looked tired and he blinked rapidly – a nervous tic. Leaning forward he said, "My own doctor will examine you and prepare a poultice for your head. Tomorrow you'll be up again. There is a lot of work to be done and you must get fit. Rose might be on his way to Jhansi, but so is Tantia Topey. Your friend here," he indicated Saleem, "has just brought word that Tantia is advancing with more than 20,000 men! Of course we can win! After all, that was the destiny predicted for my beloved child." His voice rose as he quoted some Sanskrit verses from the Rani's horoscope: "She will rise like a star lights the midnight sky and shatter her enemies into smithereens."

The Rani's father got up. "I trained her in the art of warfare, gave her the gift of a military education, made her into a man, swallowing the taunts of kith and kin, all so she would serve her country, not turn tail like a hyena. No, never," he added proudly. "Jhansi belongs to Rani Lakshmibai. *Jai* to the Rani! Victory to her!" were his last words as he walked out of the stables and back towards the palace.

The die was cast.

A few days later, posters were seen all over Jhansi and the surrounding area, which read:

Maharani Lakshmibai Devi calls on all her loyal citizens.
    The English are coming, but they will be destroyed, just as they have tried to destroy our Hindu faith and the faith of our Muslim brothers. They have desecrated the sacred right of Hindu wives to be burnt on their husbands' funeral pyres. They have forced widows to re-marry, against all the

injunctions of scripture. They have exalted all converts to the Christian religion. They have mixed bones of cows with flour and forced soldiers to use cartridges greased with pig fat.

Death to the English!

March–April 1858

Saleem was singing his new song while we packed up our few possessions:

What is life compared to honour
What is life compared to courage
What is her life compared to her Jhansi?

He threw his disguises into an old piece of yellow cloth, which became a pouch when you gathered up its four corners. "I reckon we won't be needing these for a while," Saleem said.

"Why not?" I asked.

"I don't know, just a hunch. Who knows where you and I will be next month or next year?"

"Riding with the other sowars of *Hotey ka Paltan*."

"Huh, I'm not so sure."

I looked at him quizzically. Before, he had always been so sure about his future. But that morning, on 20 March, Rani Lakshmibai had presided over several councils of war. Plans had been drawn up for the coming battle and what to do in the event of defeat. The Rani gave explicit instructions to everyone. My brother, Sewak Singh, elevated to Colonel rank, was responsible for the Rani's safety and that of her son. In the event of disaster he knew exactly what to do – have her mare ready and saddled, with provision pouch and crown jewels handy, bring Damodar Rao on horseback to wherever the Rani might be and whisk them out of harm's way to the town of Kalpi. That was just one of his responsibilities. Each of us was assigned a task and we rehearsed it step by step.

I was so proud of my brother. From a lowly sepoy, he had risen in the space of a year to a cavalry officer, and the most trusted of the Rani's advisers; no, more than adviser, her friend. I felt that some of his glory seemed to have rubbed off on me as well.

"We are moving from the palace to the fort," the Rani told Saleem and me in a private audience that same morning. "Saleem, I hear that you have found someone whose pigeons can carry messages to our allies? Tantia Topey is on his way to help us, together with the Rajas of Banpur and Shahgarh. I want you to set up the pigeon service – it will be invaluable once fighting begins. You, Hanuman, are entrusted with Prince Damodar Rao's safety, which is to be guarded at all costs. That means his life is more important than yours – you must shield it whatever happens."

Nursemaid again! Saleem shot me a look to which I didn't react with even as much as a blink. The Rani considered me shrewdly. "If I fall in battle – which is more than likely – Damodar Rao becomes the Raja of Jhansi, except the English will not recognize his title because he is adopted. He'll fight for his hereditary rights and will need a wise and loyal friend at his side. You. It should be an honour, Hanuman, so ensure my wishes are carried out." With a quick movement, she pulled the rope of pearls that hung on her chest over her head and held it out to me – a satiny waterfall of precious stones. "Take this, and remember our meeting today. Everything is poised on a great wave of change. This necklace will be a constant in your life. Go on, take it. Remember how Lord Rama's wife, Sita, gave her pearls to the monkey god, Hanuman? He had helped to rescue her from the demon, Ravana. You will do the same for me, I know."

Something stuck in my throat, a lump that wouldn't dissolve, however much I tried to swallow. All my feelings of love and loyalty for the Rani seemed to be caught in that lump, which was about to betray me… I clenched my fist to stop those tears forming, and waited until the blood started to find its natural flow again. "I will serve you, Highness, for as long as I live," I vowed. The Rani touched my head briefly with her fingers and dismissed us.

Round-the-clock preparations had begun for the defence of Jhansi from the armies of Generals Rose and Whitlock. Labourers worked in relays, filling sandbags, then carrying them either manually or on donkeys, to form a continuous breast-high wall around the city. My brother guessed that the main attack would come from the south, since the west and east were pretty much impossible to breach, protected as they were by natural rock and the city wall. Once the sandbags were in place, the men were told to keep them watered and damp, in order to absorb the impact of the English heavy guns. Stocks of wheat and rice and vegetables were hurriedly brought in, but water was no problem because there was a small reservoir inside the fort itself.

The meagre number of our troops, including the women soldiers, were busy drilling, polishing arms and armour and learning their positions. From time to time, I saw brief glimpses of Sewak Singh as he rushed about, frantically checking that everything was orderly and in place. I had never imagined that a man could drive himself so hard and for so long.

My brother stopped briefly beside me, in the midst of his preparations. I noticed that his hair was streaked with white, although he was only in his twenties. He said bitterly, "We are going to be sitting ducks, but that's what the generals and Moro Pant have decided for the Rani. We should take the initiative and attack the English before they come any nearer. How do we know what Tantia's men are like? They could be simple countrymen and peasants. The generals say that he will outflank the English army with his 22,000 men, but a surprise attack now will be worth twice that strength."

Damodar Rao played with his toy soldiers for hours every day, since lessons, athletics and riding were all indefinitely suspended. He demanded my company as he manoeuvred his troops, and we arranged and rearranged his armies until I was really bored with letting him win spectacularly every time. I often had to remind myself of my promise to his mother.

Early on the evening of 23 March we watched General Rose's army moving towards us from our positions on the ramparts of the outer fort. A sickle moon hung in the sky like a curved blade and the dull, red granite of the fort breathed out the day's heat. I marvelled at the neatness of the enemy's formation, as it progressed steadily towards us in the blue haze. They stopped about a quarter of a mile short of the city and struck camp. Then, after a short interval, seven sets of cavalry arranged themselves in a semi-circular attacking position. Not one of us slept that night, knowing that the battle was about to begin. At dawn, we saw bonfires sparking, throwing up billows of smoke to disguise movement, and our soldiers started to fire.

The enemy answered with cannon fire. The first shots thudded harmlessly against the walls of the fort. A spurt of smoke followed by a whistling noise came at odd intervals. It was like a children's game. Then, suddenly, it gathered intensity with a shower of gunfire popping like seedpods in a forest fire.

I watched, well beyond the range of the enemy. On that first day, I even brought the prince out of his hidey-hole to watch with me, giving him a blow-by-blow account of what was going on. "Look, Highness, the English are not wearing red coats. They have a new khaki uniform, which makes them harder to pick out." All at once, the Rani was there beside us, with a face like thunder.

"Are you out of your mind?" she shouted. "Take him indoors – at once!"

She was working like fury – directing soldiers, firing, encouraging, scolding, all from the white turret on the south side of the fort. Her women soldiers were fighting as bravely as the men by their side.

Our guns started answering seriously – one burst, then another, then firing almost without pause. Ghaus Khan, our Afghan artillery chief, darted here and there, amongst the squat brass guns, helping his men load and encouraging them to keep up the steady barrage. I wished that Saleem was with me, to wonder at the spectacle in the battlefield below, but he had left already to make arrangements for his pigeon post with Tantia Topey's pigeon-keeper. Tantia was said to be not more than twenty miles distant and riding hard on his way to help the Rani.

Suddenly it was evening, and then night fell like a black cloak. The day had disappeared in a mad flurry of activity. On both sides the guns packed up, since there was little sense in wasting ammunition once darkness had camouflaged the positions of the two armies. The English didn't light any fires that night. Their men must have had to make do with iron rations.

The real offensive began early next day and with it

came the first casualties. It was my first experience of seeing men die before my eyes – shot down, wounded, bleeding and in agony. I had begged my brother to be allowed closer to the action. Once I had made sure that Sushilabai, the nurse, was guarding the prince, I was given permission to help with the wounded.

"Here, young fellow, take his legs," I was told. "That's right, gently now…"

All around, voices called out to me, "Water, water, Allah's mercy, give me a drink…"

"Rama, Rama, I'm dying, tell my mother to be kind to my wife…"

I helped where I could – carrying soldiers to the field hospital, fetching water to ease the raging thirst of the dying, comforting those beyond help. One man actually expired in my arms as I was trickling water into his mouth. I was exhausted. It was mid-afternoon now and a pall of smoke and dust hung over the enemy's positions and over the fort, making it difficult to know if it was night or day. My eardrums were throbbing from the noise of explosives. From time to time, I kept a check on Damodar Rao who was safe inside the fort. He was holding his hands clapped firmly over his ears and whimpering because his arms hurt with the effort of keeping them up.

During the week-long siege, the Rani slept barely more than ten hours altogether. Dressed plainly in men's clothes, without a single jewel or ornament, she stayed within the turret for hours. She came outside when the temperature dropped a little, when she would pace the ramparts, sheltered to some extent by the sandbags, but a target nonetheless for a determined sniper. Nathu heard a story that the English soldiers and officers admired her so much that they quite deliberately kept from picking her off. Food was brought to her, but Lakshmibai hardly ate. A large, red earthenware pot was kept topped up with water by a maid, who ladled it out to the Rani with a silver ladle. I watched her drinking greedily, wiping her mouth with the back of her hand like any common soldier.

Nathu had important news. "The attack is starting tomorrow."

The British were finding it impossible to breach the thick granite walls of the city, so the next logical step was to penetrate Jhansi by scaling the walls with ladders. Just before midnight, a shout went up from the ramparts. Someone had spotted a great orange glow on the horizon – a bonfire.

"It's Tantia Topey on his way to relieve us!" cried the Rani, overjoyed. "We shall be saved, everything will work out!"

At dawn on 3 April, we watched General Rose sweeping towards Tantia's advancing army with two brigades. We could make out that his men were outflanking Tantia and then, suddenly, what did we see? Retreat! Tantia was being driven back. We could just make out the pell-mell movement of his army disappearing to goodness knew where. Shouts of anguish went up. Abandoned! We had been left to face the attack on our own.

My brother sat with his head between his knees, the picture of despair. I could hardly believe what I saw. My brave soldier brother, who didn't know the meaning of fear, who never revealed his feelings, was bowed with grief and anger! His voice sounded like it was coming from a long way off: "A lost opportunity, Hanuman! It will never come our way again – 1,500 dead, and for nothing. Our men should have gone after the British battalions when they started to chase Tantia across the Betwa River. I told the generals that a pincer movement would weaken and scatter them, but would they listen? The Rani was in complete agreement with my plan..."

His anguished expression and blackened face made him seem like a stranger. He wiped the sweat off his brow with a filthy turban end. "That's it, we are finished now. Prepare for the end, Hanuman, and thank that senile fool, Moro Pant, for landing us in this mess. The English will overrun us any day now. Nathu says that their engineers and sappers are building ladders to scale the city walls. Worst of all, our water supply is nearly finished."

A tremendous explosion interrupted him. I guessed that it was about three or four in the morning. A soldier came running towards us. His feet were making a loud slapping sound on the stone path. He shouted, "They've breached the wall! The ladders are up!"

Sewak Singh jumped up to run to consult the Rani in the white turret, but first he put his hands on my shoulders, looking deep into my eyes with his old warmth.

"There's going to be a huge affray. We are going to stir up the greatest noise and confusion the British will ever see. It's only a sham, but there's a small chance that it may terrorize them. Protect yourself. Take cover, and if anything happens to me, Hanuman, go back home only after you have seen to the prince's needs. Tell Father to always be kind to my wife and God preserve you always." And he was gone.

Then the world went mad. Explosions, gunfire, bugles and drums all combined their dreadful power in deafening noise. Suddenly, the enemy was there! White faces and brown faces were rushing through our narrow lanes, yelling bloodthirsty cries and laying their swords about them right and left, sparing no one in their path. I shrank into a doorway, too terrified to know what to do next. All I could think of at that moment was saving my life. In total panic, I tried think of a safer place. The sun was just lighting the streets and roofs of Jhansi. Its gutters were running with blood. My promise not to desert the prince seemed completely pointless. I was in no position to help anyone, least of all myself. The noise was inhuman as the soldiers rampaged down the lane. Their bloodthirsty cries, the screams of their victims, the thud of impact, the clang of iron... I tried to shut my ears to the screams of a dying woman, as I figured out how to get back to the inner

116

fort. I was close to the palace, so maybe I could make my way over the rooftops to reach the second courtyard, next to the stables. Then I could secrete myself in the hidden tunnel that led to the eastern walls of the fort. It was my only hope. I crept inside the house, in whose doorway I'd been hiding myself, and found the stairs to the rooftop. All the rooftops were linked in one way or other, and quite quickly I found myself overlooking one of the side doors to the palace. I nearly cried with relief to see that it was open. The first courtyard was full of bodies, slashed with crimson like the sunrise. I dashed across to the second courtyard, opened the trapdoor inside the stables and collapsed on the tunnel floor, trembling and very, very frightened. Where was the prince now? Had he and his mother managed to escape? Where was Saleem? My brother? Nathu? Questions peppered my brain like gunshots, until I thought I would go mad.

My shoes, my turban and my shirt had all been lost, but I still had my life. Bit by bit, I felt my way in the darkness through the familiar passage and soon I was safely by the fort.

She had gone. Under cover of darkness, the Rani and her son had galloped off to Kalpi, just 100 miles away. She had been accompanied by her two bravest women soldiers.

"She left a message for you," Nathu told me. "Follow on if you wish." He screwed up his eyes with the effort of remembering exactly. "That's it, follow on if you wish, but only if your heart tells you to go. She left orders for a horse to be kept ready by the barracks and saddled for you. Look, Hanuman, take my advice and go home. It's all over now."

"Never," I said, ashamed and angry with my selfish behaviour. "I gave my word to my brother that I would stick by them and I am going to look for the Rani and Damodar Rao if it kills me."

Only an hour or two remained of darkness. I still don't know how I managed to escape the burning city, abandoning my brother and the fellow soldiers defending the fort. I galloped through a cordon of enemy soldiers, too busy storming the hill behind the fort to worry about one boy fleeing the battle. This was the way the Rani must have galloped through, her son clinging on to her – weaving and dodging the confusion in a clatter of hooves and flying manes.

Gradually, the clamour subsided behind me, and I started to set my mind on the journey ahead. At the same time, my confused brain registered that some double-dealing son of an owl must have exchanged the decent mount ordered for me by the Rani. This horse seemed to have some trouble galloping, and it gradually slowed to a canter. As the sun climbed higher, I started wondering if I would ever reach my destination. I hadn't met a soul on the way, so I couldn't ask for directions, but just kept going by guesswork. A couple of hours on, I knew I was lost.

I'd taken a track which was leading us deeper and deeper into a thickly wooded forest. How I prayed and prayed to meet another human being who could direct me to Kalpi! Then, trotting with difficulty, the horse stumbled over a tree root and I fell, hitting my head against something very hard.

When I came to, the day had nearly ended. There was no sign of the horse and my arm felt as though I'd never be able to use it again. My food and water were in a saddlebag strapped to the horse. My throat was parched and my mouth felt like a sparrow's nest. "I'm going to die of hunger and thirst in this jungle," I thought. Then my mind shot to my brother, and I worried frantically if he would survive the battle for Jhansi. Saleem – what had happened to him since that disastrous retreat of Tantia Topey? He'd gone to set up his pigeon service, which had turned out to be a useless task, because Jhansi had been abandoned. Then I remembered the Rani's pearls, which were hidden in an inner pocket of my jacket. If I was found by thugs or bandits in this jungle, they would be sure to murder me for the priceless gems. Where could I hide them, where I could recover them again? To my huge relief, just a few yards away, I spotted a sacred shrine. Inside the hollow of a *sal* tree, the tribal forest people had placed a carving of one of their gods. I dragged myself there on my bottom and put my hand in the hollow. Inside was a ledge. It was very awkward taking out the pearls, since they were in a pocket on my left and I couldn't move my right arm. But I managed somehow and, wrapping them in a *tendu* leaf, placed them on the ledge, before memorizing the location of the tree. It was where the path branched in several directions like the points of a star. After that, I don't remember much, as I must have fainted again.

When I opened my eyes, it was morning and I was looking into the face of a young woman, who was splashing water on to my cracked lips. I thought she must have been a forest dweller gathering firewood, but she spoke in a very refined way in my dialect. "I thought you had dropped out of the sky!"

"No, I came on a horse. It's wandered off

somewhere. I have to get to Kalpi, and urgently," I croaked.

"Why, what's your hurry?" she said. "Don't you know that there are robbers and soldiers and armies all over the place? The world is very dangerous."

"Exactly." Her face was kind and her eyes were compassionate. I don't know what made me trust her, but maybe she had been sent as the answer to my fervent prayers. "I have to find the Rani of Jhansi and take my instructions from her."

"Why, is she in Kalpi? We heard that she was fighting for her city."

"Lost. Defeated," I said.

The young woman was silent, considering what I had told her. Her glass bangles clinked as she moved her arm to adjust her head covering. They reminded me of my little sister! My mind flashed weeks back to the *Bhai-dooj* fair and how I had bought bangles for her. The woman before me was thinking. Again, I wondered who she was and what she was doing in the forest, but before I could form a question, she asked, "What's your name?"

"Hanuman Singh of Digna."

The woman's eyes lit up and to my utter astonishment she added quietly, "Son of Thakur

Channa Singh and brother of Sepoy Sewak Singh?" Then she started to laugh and for a minute I thought her laughter was turning to sobs. "God is indeed great." She wiped her eyes. "My name is Maria, sister of Christopher and daughter of Aminabai and Hamid Khan of Digna."

The woman was Saleem's sister!

May – June 1858

I already knew that Saleem's older sister, Maria, whose birth name was Bilquis Fatima, worked as an *ayah* for Mr and Mrs Fenton of Nowgaon, looking after their two children. She had been earning her living since the age of fourteen, and now she must be seventeen or eighteen. Maria and the four Fentons had all managed to escape from the rebel sepoys and found refuge with a friendly woodcutter in the jungle for the past month. There was still a danger from Thakurs, bandits and villagers who were hunting for white fugitives to win themselves hefty rewards. Maria and her employers were waiting for General Rose's forces to establish control over the locality before showing themselves in public.

It was these English fugitives who saved my life, fed me and watered me and bound up my arm. For two weeks I stayed in their forest camp, as a friend from Maria's village.

"Don't tell them anything about who you are, or your connection to the Rani. You know that they will hang her when they catch her. Let's say your name is Saleem. You are a cousin from my village and you were travelling to see your wife."

"My wife! I'm not even married."

Maria looked mischievously at me. "So what? Lots of boys of your age have been married for two years or more. You and I could always get married, but you are too young for me." She had the same wicked sense of humour as Saleem, and that made me miss him even more. As soon as I could ride again, I thought, I would leave for Kalpi. Luckily, my horse had wandered back into the camp.

Maria told me that many of the locals were sheltering and protecting English people. Certainly the Fentons, her employers, were very kind to me, even though they made me join them in their Christian prayers, morning, noon and night. The saddest thing of all was that I couldn't give Maria any news of her brother, although I told her over and over again about all the adventures we had shared together.

My arm had mended nicely when, in the middle of May, a tribal forest dweller came rushing into our clearing with the news that the British army had taken Kalpi. He also said that the Rani of Jhansi had ridden to Gwalior to mount an offensive against the British with Tantia and Rao Sahib – Nana Sahib's nephew. I couldn't wait to join her. It was time for me to go.

"Send word to me about Saleem," Maria whispered. She arranged for a tribal man to lead me and my horse to the forest edge and to point me in the direction of Gwalior. On my way, I stopped at the crossroads in the forest and retrieved the Rani's pearls from the hollow tree.

The Gwalior Fort is a hundred times more impressive than the fort in Jhansi. It was built centuries ago and looms on the very edge of an enormous ledge of rock, hundreds of feet above the winding, dusty road below. It's nearly two miles in length and a mile in width. Five gateways stand guard and it looks as though nothing could possibly destroy it.

By the time I arrived, the Rani, Tantia Topey and Nana Sahib's nephew, Rao Sahib, were already established there. Tantia had managed to win over Scindia's army, which everyone had supposed to be completely loyal to Maharajah Scindia of Gwalior. The Maharajah, in turn, had fled to Agra to hide behind the skirts of the British. Even after their defeats in

Jhansi and Kalpi, the Rani and her allies still thought that they had a chance of driving the British from Bundelkhand. They were in command of a great stronghold and now they also had a huge, well-trained army and plenty of money from the Scindia treasury. I learned all this in due course from Rani Lakshmibai, whose face lit up when she saw me arrive in her chambers in Gwalior Fort.

"Oh, Hanuman, I am so happy to see you alive and well! I thought we had lost you! My news is only tragic. Hanuman, they are all dead: my father, Moro Pant; your brave brother, Sewak Singh; Saleem, our best spy; General Ghaus Khan; my two favourite women soldiers and many, many others." Her eyes were tear-filled and her cheeks became wet.

I had never before seen the Rani cry and my heart was full of sadness, for the news of my brother and my best friend, and for her losses, too. I stifled a sob and she put her hand on my arm and pressed it gently. "I know what your brother meant to you. He died fighting like the bravest hero. Take heart and don't give up now. God has spared you for some noble task, and I need your courage to stand against these fools who I'm ashamed to call my allies. Have you heard that Rao Sahib is feasting and making merry, just because we've captured Gwalior?" She spoke shrilly, "And who is advancing on our heels? General Rose and his army. We should go out and meet them, just as Sewak Singh would have done. Instead, what are they doing? Nothing. Getting drunk and ogling dancing girls!"

There was a great change in the Rani's appearance and her manner – something nervous and brittle about her person. But I was too unhappy to worry about that.

For days and nights I grieved for my brother. I pictured all the times I had waited and watched for Sewak Singh and how I had wanted to be like him in every way. I thought about his last words to me over and over again. I forced myself to remember everything we had talked about during our last year together in Jhansi. It was terribly painful, but I didn't want to forget anything. I hoped that my parents hadn't heard the news from a stranger and wished that I were in Digna to mourn with them. But it wasn't only Sewak Singh I mourned, it was Saleem, too, the truest friend I will ever have. One of Saleem's songs played in my mind like a brain-fever bird, over and over again:

How bravely like a man she fights, the Rani of Jhansi!
Laying about her left and right, the Rani of Jhansi!
None can match her skill and might, the Rani of Jhansi!

Such an air of sadness and despair hung over us all, and the June heat brought sickness to our stomachs. The Rani stalwartly drilled her soldiers and practised manoeuvres, trying to keep them fit and alert and ready for battle. But no one else seemed to be bothered. Damodar Rao was a frightened little fellow, sallow-faced and timid. He had shed his puppy fat and missed his nurse, Sushilabai, who had also died in the battle of Jhansi.

One day, the Rani took me aside and whispered that I should take Damodar Rao back to our village until it became safe for him to return. I would have done that gladly, but all the roads south were swarming with enemy soldiers, so we decided to watch for a few more days and see what would happen.

Nathu was still around and from him I learned how my brother had died. He was part of the last band of men who defended the hill at the back of Jhansi Fort.

"They fought like tigers, Hanuman. There were only 50 or so, and there was no hope at all, but they died battling with the enemy, to the last man. Not one was taken prisoner. Sewak Singh died holding aloft the flag of Jhansi in one hand."

Two weeks after she had left for Kalpi, Lakshmibai's father was hanged by the British. Saleem was shot by a sniper as he tried to enter Jhansi. Nana Sahib had escaped to Nepal, leaving his nephew, Rao Sahib, in charge.

Bits of news filtered through, all bad. The country, apart from our area, was settling down and returning to a more peaceful state. The roads were open, the telegraph was working and law and order was being enforced by the British. Gwalior and parts of Bundelkhand were now the only territories still fighting the foreigner. Everywhere else in India the British had regained control and were busy rebuilding and establishing their rule once again. Every day, new stories were coming through. I heard about the thousands of sepoys, and anyone who had been involved in the Mutiny, that had been hanged or executed. We in Gwalior, led by the Rani, were the very last to put up any resistance, a whole year after the Mutiny had begun.

On 18 June, the air was so heavy and thick that it was an effort to breathe. Nathu crept back with news from

the enemy camp. "The *Angrez* general has got sunstroke. So have four of his senior officers. May they all perish from it." In the evening he came back from another spying mission. He told the Rani that he had seen troop movements on the road south-east of the city. Rani Lakshmibai immediately sent me with a message for Tantia and Rao Sahib with the news.

"We must post soldiers on the hilly ground between Kotah-ki-Serai and the city. Even more importantly, we have to take the initiative and attack the English as they advance."

Tantia sent a note back saying that he was all for an engagement, but Rao Sahib was not so confident. "Tell your mistress that we should wait a few more days. Perhaps if the rains come we'll have a better chance to attack. We know the lie of the land, but they will depend on roads, which could become rivers of mud…"

When I informed the Rani, she jumped up, shouting angrily, "We should have been prepared for this advance by the British. That fool, Rao Sahib. I have been talking myself hoarse for the past fortnight, but he was too busy amusing himself with his wine and women to listen to me. Now I am going to do as I think fit."

She prepared herself for the final battle. Never will that scene be erased from my mind.

She gave orders that her battledress should be laid out. It was a red jacket and trousers. She fastened heavy gold anklets around her slender ankles, then slipped the Scindia pearls over her neck and tied a black bandana around her head. In her belt, she wore a pistol decorated with mother-of-pearl and her sword hung from her waist. The priest arrived to bless her, circling her head with an oil lamp and imprinting a thumbmark of saffron paste and rice on her forehead. He chanted some prayers and bowed low. Damodar Rao was brought to say goodbye to his mother and he clung to her in a most pathetic way. I cannot describe how I felt. It was as though I were sleepwalking, as though the scene before me was a bad dream. I remember pinching myself, but I was awake after all. It was clear to me and everyone else in the room that we would probably not see her alive again.

"Goodbye, Hanuman. Look after my son. Take him away now; get him away from Gwalior in one of your disguises. Guard him with your life until someone comes to fetch him from your village." It took superhuman strength to hold back the tears that were welling up in her eyes. She thrust a pouch of gold coins in my hand, and then was gone. Her column of sowars and sepoys streamed out of the main fort gate, clattering with noisy hooves down the approach road and stirring up a great cloud of dust, which swirled and eddied around them.

Straightaway, I saddled my mare, because all the servants seemed to have vanished, and hoisted up the prince in front of me, so I could protect him. My heart thudded with fear and anxiety, and my damp shirt stuck to my back. We started off slowly, down the dusty road that led from Gwalior Fort to the plain. It was late in the afternoon, and away to our west, on the rocky hillside that led to Kotah-ki-Serai, our army had gathered like a dark storm cloud. Peering into the distance, I just made out the Rani's blood-coloured battledress. Her yellow and red royal banner was like a pinch of pepper against the pale sky. About half a mile from our cavalry and foot-soldiers, the British army was massing, like a heavy surge of flood water; I could see that fresh batches of riders and infantry were moving up from their base camp. It was going to be impossible to get through the enemy lines – it would simply be asking for death, and I didn't want to die or risk the prince's life.

I panicked, looking right and left, above and below for inspiration. The fort seemed to have emptied and there was no one at hand, which left the two of us even more exposed. All of a sudden, I heard someone calling my name and there, scrambling down the rocks, I saw Nathu running towards us. I almost collapsed with relief.

"Have you gone mad?" Nathu shouted angrily, grabbing the bridle. "Why are you waiting here like a sitting duck? Our army is going to be slaughtered and they'll be after the prince in no time. You're well within their range. Come on, let's get the devil out of this cursed place. Get off that horse and take off your fancy clothes, both of you."

Nathu took charge. He slapped the horse on the rump and sent it galloping in the opposite direction. Then he tipped the contents of his bag on to the ground. In the shelter of a stumpy thorn bush, the prince and I quickly changed into a disguise of rags and each wound a scanty turban round our heads. "Come on, now. We have to hide until it's dark before we can get far away from the battlefield," Nathu urged.

Just then, the distant roar of charging armies – full-throated battle cries and thundering hooves – hit our ears. Nathu pushed us down behind a huge rock and we crouched there, my arm around the prince's shoulders. The cries grew louder and fiercer, travelling across the dry atmosphere, and the clang of metal on metal rang through the air. I peered around our shelter and, although we were a good quarter of a mile away, I could see what was happening as the sun sank, red and angry, lower and lower into the horizon.

The Rani's red jacket was here, there and everywhere. I thought I saw the glint of her sword flashing. Her soldiers were hopelessly outnumbered, but still they regrouped and charged the enemy soldiers.

The sweat stood out on Nathu's forehead as he screwed up his eyes, shading them with his hand and following the action with intense concentration. As the light became dimmer, I found it difficult to see clearly, because my eyes are not that strong. Instead, I listened intently to Nathu's running commentary, trying at the same time to comfort the prince, who was crying.

Nathu said excitedly, "She's fighting with her pistol in one hand and the sword in the other. That's her style… *Jai Maharani ki!*" he exclaimed. "Long may she live!" Then his voice suddenly dropped. "Look, Hanuman!" I peered into the dusk. Her red jacket was only just visible to me. A flash of lightning seemed to travel towards her. "That swine of an Englishman!" Nathu gasped. He whispered, "She's down. I can't see her any more." A cloud of dust and gunfire smoke was making visibility even more difficult. We watched and watched and waited to spot the red jacket again, but we saw something else which made my heart sink – our soldiers seemed to be faltering and scattering in all directions.

Nathu suddenly seemed to realize where he was. "Come on, quickly, Hanuman. We've got to find a better hiding place. The British will be here to take the fort and we must not be seen."

"But what about the Rani? We have to see to her!"

"We can't risk our lives now."

I turned away unwillingly, holding tightly to the prince's hand as we stumbled in the inky darkness towards a safe haven.

Somehow, Nathu, Damodar Rao and I got away safely that terrible night. Creeping from rock to rock, we slowly found our way to a shepherd's hut. From there, we walked under cover of darkness to a village. When I last looked back at Gwalior, I could see dark shapes galloping up the hill towards the fort. In the dawn, another fugitive arrived in the village where we were sheltering and told us that the British had conquered Gwalior and that the Rani and her brave soldiers lay dead on the battlefield below. He told us how he had played dead under a heap of bloody bodies.

"I could hardly breathe with their weight. The stink of blood and death nearly choked me. There was this uncanny silence, except for the low moans of the dying. Then I heard a terrible death rattle and an English voice said, 'She was the bravest and the best,' and I knew that our heroine, our Rani, had departed this life. I waited until they came to take away the corpses and then I ran as if the devils of hell were behind me. But first, I paid my last respects to the Rani."

I didn't tell the prince about his mother until we were safely home, a few days later, and when my own mother and sisters could give him comfort.

Some months later, I heard another first-hand account of the last battle and it was unbearably painful to listen to the account of the Rani's end. She was wounded by an English officer on horseback. A strike from a sword sent her pistol flying out of her hand. Then, an English officer took aim and fired at her back. Her sword was still active, but her strength suddenly went and she fell off her horse. A great cry went up, echoing round the battlefield: "*Jhansi ki Rani katal ki gayi! Jhansi ki Rani zinda rahegi!*" The Rani of Jhansi has been killed! Long live the Rani of Jhansi! Apparently, General Rose himself had stood over her as she lay dying and said, "She was the bravest and the best."

Once she was gone, the fight went out of Rao Sahib and his soldiers. Even though Tantia wandered the countryside for months, troubling the English with guerrilla warfare, effectively the Mutiny was over. The soldier who told me this story said that the Rani had whispered a message to be sent to me: "The pearls are for his wife. Tell him never to leave my son." She had wanted Nathu to have her gold anklets. Her Scindia pearls were entrusted to the soldier, who put them into my hands for Damodar Rao.

Epilogue 1859

Prince Damodar Rao lived with my family for many months and became a strong and healthy boy, but he never spoke much again. He went to the village school, played with my little sister and liked hearing stories from me about his brave mother. I am not ashamed to say that each time I talked about her, I had to restrain my tears.

The following year, his relatives came to our village and took Damodar Rao back to Jhansi, to be educated and brought up like a prince. Nathu took over my job as *khidmutgar*. As for me, the thought of going back to the place that had once been like a fairytale, but had turned into a nightmare, made me sick. I became so ill that my parents insisted I break my promise to the late Rani. I knew that I would be too unhappy and sad to be a good companion to the prince. And, although I felt that I had betrayed him and his mother, I also knew that I wouldn't be able to bear to return to Jhansi Palace.

I remained behind in Digna to lead a quiet life.

My old dream of becoming a soldier had gone, never to return. Instead I set my mind to learning about farming, being an obedient son and finishing my schooling with the village priest.

Historical note

The definition of *mutiny* in the Oxford dictionary is: "open revolt against constituted authority, especially by soldiers, etc, against officers." However, in the history of India, the Mutiny (sometimes called the Sepoy Mutiny) carried much greater weight than is allowed in the dictionary meaning, and its significance went far beyond a military rebellion. Many Indian historians and nationalists renamed and redefined it as the First War of Independence. Much later, Indians regarded the series of violent uprisings between 1857–58 to be the first widespread uprising against foreign rule; and it is clear that in those unsettled times many sections of the Indian people seized the opportunity to express their anger and frustration against the British.

The British relationship with India started as long ago as 1600, when Europeans started exploring the East for spices. The Portuguese, Dutch and French competed with the British to establish market domination over southern Asia, and the British eventually became the super-power in India. The British "East India Company" established three main trading stations: Calcutta, Bombay and Madras. India was the golden land of opportunity and adventure, and many British traders, such as Robert Clive and Warren Hastings, succeeded in making enormous fortunes for themselves. The strength of the East India Company's army and administration enabled the British to take over large tracts of land and to annex kingdom after local kingdom.

In the eighteenth century, India was a mosaic of states, some being part of larger provinces, such as Bundelkhand. Some states were ruled by Hindu Rajas, Ranis, Maharajahs or Maharanis (*maha* means "great") and some by Muslim Nawabs and Begums. An enormous part of northern India was ruled by the Mughal Emperor, but a large part of western, central and southern India came under Maratha rule. Under Mughal and Maratha rule, individual Indian states were allowed to keep their own rulers and armies, and retain their autonomy.

But from the mid-eighteenth century, as the Mughal Empire grew weaker, some state rulers began to look to the British Governor General for protection from neighbouring rivals. They gained a British presence in their territories, but lost their autonomy. The Larai Rani of Orchha was one of these. Others who defied the foreigner were branded as dangerous and disloyal, and displaced, like the Marathas in the west. In the 50 years between 1799 and 1849, the British had taken over much of southern India, half of the northern state of Oudh, the kingdom of the Marathas in the west, the kingdom of the Sikhs in Punjab (Panjab), as well as the province of Sind. New laws were formulated to ban traditions such as widow-burning (*sati*), and ritual robbery and murder (*thugee*). Missionaries took the gospel message all over the country, and there was great nervousness and fear that the British intended to forcibly convert Indians to Christianity.

A high percentage of soldiers in the Bengal Army, as the main British military force was called, came from farming backgrounds. Hindus in the army belonged to the higher castes and, although Indian soldiers were not allowed to become officers, it was still an attractive job with a regular salary and prestige. The British administration had been clumsy and insensitive in applying land tax and forcing farmers to grow cash crops, which were unprofitable in the long run. Many severe famines led to great hardship among peasants and landowners (Thakurs). Soldiers knew the difficult conditions at first hand, since their own families were affected. Undercurrents of resentment simmered under the surface calm.

Then again, a large proportion of the Bengal Army consisted of natives of Oudh and the surrounding region. In their view, even if the ruler, the Nawab of Oudh, was corrupt and ineffectual, he was still their ruler. The ease with which the British took over Oudh and other wealthy kingdoms created another cauldron of bitterness.

Until the 1820s, soldiers and white officers shared an easy camaraderie and mutual respect, but the younger generation now arriving from Britain were less considerate and well-mannered. Indian soldiers began to resent their arrogant behaviour. British army officers, meanwhile, had taken great pride in the loyalty and discipline of their Indian soldiers. When the Mutiny began, they could hardly believe the evidence of their men being responsible for rebellion and slaughter. Obviously, they had never imagined that "their men" would turn against them. It was partly the British paralysis of will and organization that helped the Indians to quickly gain the upper hand.

The first rumblings of the Indian Mutiny began in February 1857 in the army cantonment near Calcutta. Bullets for the new Enfield rifle were greased with pig's lard and cow fat. This was totally offensive to Muslims and Hindus alike, and though the bullets were quickly taken out of circulation, sepoys remained suspicious. Soon after, protests broke out in Behrampur and Barrackpur, and on 3 May soldiers openly revolted in Lucknow. They were disarmed and their leaders were imprisoned in Meerut. By now, rumours were rife, quickly fuelling the crisis in the army. It was said that the bones of cows had been mixed with *chapatti* flour, and that a forcible conversion campaign was about to begin. Then the mysterious *chapattis* began to circulate in the countryside, although no one has been able to accurately interpret their meaning. On other occasions *chapattis* were couriered in advance warning of a smallpox plague and other disasters, so the Mutiny *chapattis* could have also have warned of trouble ahead. But on 10 May, the Mutiny proper broke out in Meerut, when soldiers of the 3rd Light Cavalry, 11th Native Infantry and 20th Native Infantry rose up in arms. They killed their British officers, set fire to bungalows and set off for nearby Delhi.

Soon, there were 50 Europeans dead in Delhi and other mutinies broke out in all the other cantonment towns – Ferozepur, Roorkee, Aligarh, Lucknow, Benares, Kanpur, Jhansi and many other stations. The most famous siege was at Lucknow, when hundreds of British men, women and children barricaded themselves in the Residency (the home of the principal British official) until they were relieved by General Havelock and his army after three months. Europeans, Indian Christians and anyone known to be in sympathy with the British were murdered. In Delhi, the aged Mughal Emperor, Bahadur Shah, was proclaimed the king of Delhi.

Delhi was not regained by the British until the end of September 1857. Then, three sons of Bahadur Shah were shot dead by an English officer. Nearly another year was to pass (until the summer of 1858) before the British regained proper control over what they considered to be their rightful territories.

The Rani of Jhansi

Lakshmibai of Jhansi was of Maratha parentage. The Maratha were among the strongest of British opponents, but nevertheless their territories were annexed and the Peshwa's (Maratha king's) adopted son was denied his father's pension. Lakshmibai was brought up among boys – Tantia Topey and Nana Sahib, the son of the Peshwa, were her childhood companions. She was taught fighting skills and became an accomplished horsewoman. Her husband, the Raja of Jhansi, died when she was still in her twenties, leaving her to rule over the kingdom.

She is hero-worshipped as a symbol of Indian nationalism, and was greatly admired by British generals and soldiers for her fighting skills and bravery. General Rose is reputed to have said that if the Mutiny had been led by a few more Ranis like Lakshmibai, the British would never have stood a chance.

One of the problems in writing about the Mutiny is that there are hardly any written accounts from the Indian point of view. Most of what passes for fact, especially as regards Jhansi, is based on local stories and songs, and this makes the historian's task very difficult. For instance, many Indians picture the Rani leaping from the ramparts of Jhansi Fort on to her grey mare and galloping to Kalpi with her son strapped to her back. This feat would be physically impossible, because of the extreme height of the fort walls. It is difficult to contradict popular opinion without hurting people's sentiments, and it is difficult to interpret exactly what took place in the Rani's palace and her strategies. The fact that she decided to fight the British more than six months after the rebellion in Jhansi cantonment suggests that she felt her position to be very insecure. On all sides, there was the threat from neighbouring rival princes, her own soldiers, the British and even the neighbouring Thakurs. Only after realizing that the British did not trust her, did the Rani join Tantia Topey and Rao Sahib (Nana Sahib's nephew). However, all accounts of that time demonstrate her commitment to her kingdom and her cause; of her courage in battles there is no doubt at all. That she died a heroine's death has never been in dispute.

After the Mutiny

Once the Mutiny had been quelled, the ancient Mughal Emperor Bahadur Shah was exiled to Burma and Tantia Topey was hanged. Less than twenty years later, in 1876, Queen Victoria was made Empress of India. The East India Company was disbanded and India became the responsibility of a department of Whitehall in London. The British government (*Raj*) was now firmly in place over almost the entire subcontinent and a Viceroy was appointed in true Imperial tradition.

But within the short space of 90 years, Indians gathered their forces under the leadership of exceptional men and women. Great nationalists and patriots such as Mahatma Gandhi and Jawaharlal Nehru inspired ordinary Indians to struggle against British rule and demand their freedom.

In August 1947, the British left India after a tremendous battle of wills. The result was two nations, India and Pakistan. In 1971, Bangladesh broke away from Pakistan. Where there was one country, there are now three independent nations.

Timeline

1757 Battle of Plassey. The British, under the command of Robert Clive, win a decisive victory over the Nawab of Bengal. This established the rule of the East India Company and the power of the British over other Europeans in India.

1799 Battle of Seringapatam opens the way to British control over southern India.

1818 Defeat of the Marathas in western India.

1848–49 Annexation of Punjab.

1857–59 The First War of Independence, or the Mutiny.

1858 Disbandment of the East India Company. India is now under direct British rule.

1876 Queen Victoria proclaimed Empress of India.

1947 Indian independence and the creation of West and East Pakistan (later to become Bangladesh in 1971).

The Mutiny

January 1857 Sepoys in Dum-Dum (near Calcutta) uneasy about new rifle cartridges.

10 May 1857 Mutiny begins in Meerut. Mutineers kill officers and other Europeans, and set off for Delhi.

11 May 1857 Mutineers proclaim Bahadur Shah Zafar as emperor in Delhi, and murder Europeans.

May–June 1857 Mutiny spreads all over northern India.

5–6 June 1857 Jhansi sepoys revolt.

8 June 1857 Massacre of Europeans in Jhokun Bagh.

11 June 1857 Sepoys leave Jhansi for Delhi.

27 June 1857 Massacre at Kanpur.

20 September 1857 Delhi reconquered by British after fierce fighting.

21 September 1857 Captain Hodson captures the Mughal King Bahadur Shah and murders his three sons.

13 October 1857 Two Mughal princes tried and shot.

17 November 1857 Lucknow relieved by Sir Colin Campbell.

6 January 1858 General Sir Hugh Rose begins Central Indian campaign.

14 January 1858 Rani of Jhansi issues proclamation against British.

3 March 1858 Defeat of Rajas of Shahgarh and Banpur near Jhansi.

21 March 1858 General Rose arrives at Jhansi.

23 March 1858 Investment of Jhansi begins.

3 April 1858 Jhansi captured and sacked.

5 April 1858 Jhansi Fort taken. Rani of Jhansi escapes with her son.

22 May 1858 Battle of Kalpi. Rani of Jhansi leaves for Gwalior.

1 June 1858 Rani Lakshmibai, Tantia Topey and Rao Sahib capture Gwalior.

17 June 1858 Battle of Kotah-ki-Serai. Rani of Jhansi killed in combat.

November 1858 All East India Company territories vested in Queen Victoria's name. Proclamation abolishing the East India Company.

April 1859 Tantia Topey hanged by the British.

Glossary

Ayah – nanny or nursemaid

Bajra – millet; a coarse grain used in flat bread

Batta – bonus

Bhaiya – brother

Bhaji – fried snack

Burqa – overall covering, usually black, worn by Muslim ladies

Caste – a Hindu is born into one of the four prescribed castes. Those born "outside" a caste used to be given the terrible name of untouchable

Chapatti – flat round bread made without yeast

Dal – lentils; a dish made from lentils

Diwali – Hindu festival of lights

Diya – small earthenware lamp

Dupatta – woman's head covering, sometimes worn only over the shoulders

Durbar room – audience chamber

Dussehra – Hindu festival just before *Diwali* which commemorates the victory of good over evil

Ganesh – a Hindu god

Gulli-danda – game played with two teams, a wooden spindle, and a bat

Haldi Kunku – Hindu festival celebrated in western India

Hubble-bubble – a smoking pipe, kept cool by a small water bowl

Kaffir – non-Muslim

Kharif – the autumn crop

Lassi – cooling drink made with yoghurt and water

Maharajah/Maharani – king/queen

Maidan – large open space

Mohur – gold coin

Nawab – Muslim ruler

Padshah (or Badshah) – king

Peshwa – Maratha king

Puja – worship

Raj – rule

Raja/Rani – king/queen

Ramayana – the great Hindu epic poem

Rissaldar – sergeant

Sahib/Memsahib – title usually used for white people

Sapper – soldiers who do engineering work

Sepoy – foot soldier

Shaitan – devil

Sowar – cavalry soldier

Syce – servant who looks after horses

Picture acknowledgements

P154   Lakshmibai, Rani of Jhansi, Add Or 1896, The British Library

P155   Map of Central India, András Bereznay

P156   Military firearms, Mary Evans Picture Library

P157   Nana Sahib, Hulton Deutsch Collection Ltd

P158   A group of mutineers at Lucknow, Topham Picturepoint

P158   Sepoys of the light company, 65th Bengal Native Infantry,
              J Harris after Henry Martens, Courtesy of the Director,
              National Army Museum, London

P159   Ruins at Lucknow, Topham Picturepoint

Rani Lakshmibai of Jhansi.

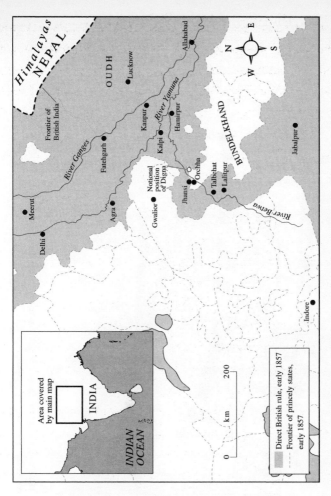

This map shows many of the places mentioned in this book. The map also shows how some parts of India were ruled directly by the British and some (the princely states) were still ruled by Indian royalty.

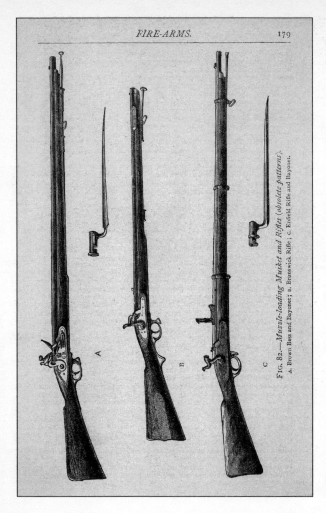

FIG. 82.—*Muzzle-loading Musket and Rifles (obsolete patterns).*
A. Brown Bess and Bayonet; B. Brunswick Rifle; C. Enfield Rifle and Bayonet.

Military firearms used in India: a) Brown Bess and bayonet, b) Brunswick rifle and c) Enfield rifle and bayonet.

An illustration of Nana Sahib and his escort leaving Lucknow during the Mutiny.

A group of mutineers at Lucknow.

Sepoys of the light company, 65th Bengal Native Infantry.

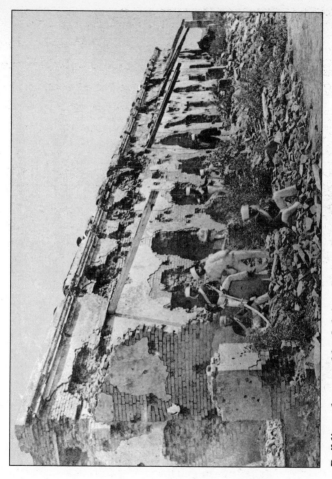

Buildings destroyed by fighting during the Mutiny at Lucknow.

Also in the series:

BATTLE OF BRITAIN
The Story of Harry Woods
England 1939-1940

THE TRENCHES
The Story of Billy Stevens
The Western Front 1914-1918

CIVIL WAR
The Story of Thomas Adamson
England 1643-1650

TRAFALGAR
The Story of James Grant
HMS Norseman 1799-1806

ARMADA
The Story of Thomas Hobbs
England 1587-1588

CRIMEA
The Story of Michael Pope
110th Regiment 1853-1857

ZULU WAR
The Story of Jabulani
Africa 1879-1882